# MISTRESS OF DARKNESS

### DREDTHORNE HALL BOOK 2

## HAZEL HUNTER

## HH ONLINE

Hazel loves hearing from readers!
You can contact her at the links below.

Website: hazelhunter.com

Facebook:
business.facebook.com/HazelHunterAuthor

Newsletter: HazelHunter.com/news

I send newsletters with details on new
releases, special offers, and other bits of
news related to my writing. You can sign
up here!

## CHAPTER 1

*N*othing had ever been good enough for Regina; not even her fiancée. As Gwen listened to the soft clapping of the horse's hooves against the packed snow, she reviewed her sister's cryptic letter again. Its meaning was clear, even if it was lacking in the thousand specifics Gwen would have liked: Regina had run away from home. Her betrayal still carried a razor edge of pain. Her sister had run away mere weeks before the elaborate wedding that Gwen and her mother had spent months planning, preparing, and slaving over. She wasn't merely thoughtless. Regina was *ungrateful*. Gwen would have done anything for the beautiful, white-and-crystalline celebration that she and her mother had devoted so many countless hours to making possible.

"Regina, where are you?" she whispered into the growing country darkness.

The crisp air, with a few gently pirouetting snowflakes, made the jingling of the halter sing all the clearer in Gwen's ears. The sound reminded her not of Christmas, but of the tiny, sparkling bells that they had imported from Paris specifically for her absent sister's nuptials. Gwen had been looking forward, with a tinge of jealousy, to the sound of so many bells ringing while Regina and Christopher walked down the aisle. Now, all that Gwen had to look forward to was the dread responsibility of her current mission. Gwen, older and only sister, now carried the weight of telling poor Christopher that his willful bride had become wayward.

Gwen sighed, closing her eyes, trusting the horse to do its work. The loss of her sister was almost too much for her to bear. Regina had been a constant presence in Gwen's life, and she had never thought that they would be apart. They would marry and live in the same town, see each other every Sunday for dinner, raise their children together...

*I do not know who I am anymore,* Regina had written in a wobbly script. *But I know that I cannot be with Christopher, not now. Perhaps not ever.*

If there was a hideous truth behind her words, Regina's parting message did not specify it. Gwen's own letter to Christopher avoided telling him any of the dire news.

*Please, meet me, sir. I need to speak with you about my sister and my family as soon as can be arranged.*

Gwen's note was enigmatic, perhaps, but it wouldn't be right to tell Christopher the crushing news in any other way than in person. She had at least been able to summon that much courage.

She peered ahead and spied Dredthorne Hall looming in the distance. The house was foreboding, a large harbinger of doom, if the rumors from town were to be believed. Gwen knew some of the details of the place already. It was of overwhelming size, with fifty-eight rooms and four floors, and was one of the oldest halls in the region. Gwen spared a thought for the poor staff that would have to keep the house. It reminded her of an aged lady of class and manners who had once been beautiful in her prime. While the overarching structure was still there, the details were fading into the background, overwhelmed by time, decay, and inevitability.

How the Sheratons came to own it or what exactly they planned to do with the place was less clear to Gwen. She had avoided the family prior to the engagement due to the poor manners of Christopher's older brother, Robert. She hoped that her mission to Christopher could be completed without having to deal with that ogre. It was fortunate that Regina had found a match with such a worthy family, but that did not mean Gwen had to like her new brother-in-law. Her mind hurried to correct the detail: the man who could have become a brother-in-law had Regina not vanished into the night with little more than a crumpled piece of paper left behind.

The rig rolled past the gate, the gentle beat of hooves on snow being replaced by the clack against brick. Stately twin lions carved from Italian marble sat atop pedestal columns and seemed to gaze down on her in disapproval. Gray slate roofs capped the soft buff stone of the house. Two towers flanked it, as though it were a small castle. The closer she got, the higher its weathered facade rose, along with her anxiety. Gwen took a deep breath as she slowed the rig to a stop. She was up to this task, she assured herself, for she had to be. There was simply no escape from it, short of finding her lost sister.

A footman approached and held out his hand to help her. She took it, lifting her dress as she stepped down, and it took everything in her to keep her face agreeable at the sight that greeted her. In that moment, she desperately wished that her home was close enough to Dredthorne Hall for her to return this evening, but *nothing* was close to Dredthorne Hall.

Robert Sheraton, Christopher's elder brother, stood tall in the midst of a small army of servants, with no Christopher in sight. The older brother's dark hair and eyes matched his somber dress. He wore a white shirt, cravat, and waist coat, accompanied by a black jacket and trousers.

Gwen had the prudence to withhold the groan that he inspired. There was nothing about Robert that appealed to her. He was prickly, quick to speak his anger, easy to enrage, and condescending. Robert made friends with no one, and had always seemed to prefer it that way. She watched as he tucked a strand of black hair behind his ear and his movement reminded her of her own appearance. She smoothed her skirts and tried to stand taller as she approached him.

Hiding her displeasure as best she could, as she had been trained, Gwen said, "Mr. Sheraton, to what do I owe this pleasure?"

With satisfaction, she noted that she had managed to sound the perfect picture of politeness. If Robert could find anything disagreeable in their meeting, it would not be her words.

He cleared his throat, smoothing a

minuscule wrinkle along his coat, and bowed slightly.

"Miss Archer. How wonderful to see you," he said with a deep voice that was suited to his large frame. But she wondered if anything he spoke besides her name was true, remembering their last encounter, in her youth. "My brother has not yet arrived from London. He asked that you remain here to await his presence in order to personally receive your....*news*." The last word was said with distaste, but she was pleasantly surprised to find the rest of his words kind in tone.

How strange, Gwen thought, examining him. It was unlike Robert to be anything but reticent and rude. No doubt he was making an extra effort, now that he thought they were to be brother and sister-in-law. Yet that would not be like him either. He'd always been one to act as he saw fit, regardless of its effect on others. She would have to watch this new Robert to see if his manners were brought upon by some unknown illness or a true change of heart.

Naturally Dredthorne Hall gave her

chills, both from its appearance and its legends. There were rumors that ghosts lingered within its confines, haunting their unfortunate victims into insanity, or even worse. The prospect of spending a night in an old house was hardly appealing. But spending a night in Dredthorne with Robert? When Regina returned she would owe Gwen a lifetime of apologies.

"How unfortunate about your brother," she said finally. "I had hoped to speak with him as soon as possible." She surveyed the servants lined up beside the elder Sheraton, the sight of them distracting her from what she could only call a vexed mood. She'd never lived in the grand style in which Robert had apparently been raised. But she swore to herself she would not appear overly impressed or act like a country simpleton. Though she might have to submit to his acting as her host, she did not have to ingratiate herself. She offered him a courteous smile. "I am certain that we will be able to find ways to entertain ourselves until he arrives."

Robert gestured toward the rig, and two footmen rushed forward to fetch her luggage. "I would think that can be arranged."

Despite her intentions, Gwen had to force herself not to stare open-mouthed at the reception hall. High above them, in the vaulted ceiling overhead, cherubs and angels seemed to be descending from heaven. Gilded alabaster carvings of delicate flowers and vines framed them, glowing as though lit from within. Life-sized paintings surrounded them, no doubt important Sheraton progenitors, some of them obviously military men.

Further inside, enormous tapestries hung from floor to ceiling, some glinting with lavishly used gold and silver threads. Over-large floor vases stood in front of them and Gwen thought she spied oriental lettering depicted on them.

As the footmen approached with her trunks, Robert gestured to the left stairwell. "The maids can show you to your chambers, Miss Archer," he said smoothly. "I do hope that you find it to your liking. It has been...less touched by time."

"My thanks, Mr. Sheraton," she said lightly, trying to hide the awe that the surroundings had already inspired. But she noticed him smiling at her and had to speculate as to whether she'd succeeded at hiding her wonderment or not. She searched his dark eyes for a moment, trying to find the dismal Robert that she knew had to be buried within their depths. But instead she only saw a penetrating intensity that was rather unnerving. She looked away. "I'm sure the accommodations will be lovely. I would, however, like to send word to my family that I may be delayed."

"Of course," he said. "One of the footmen can post your letter. I would be honored if you would join me for dinner. Shall we say at seven o'clock this evening? I am sure Frances would be happy to see to any needs you might have." He gestured to a maid, who bobbed a quick curtsy. "Frances, see that Miss Archer finds her way."

But even as he spoke to the young maid, Gwen saw that he was watching her with a strange expression; something akin to pleasure combined with confusion, which made no sense at all to her.

Gwen nodded to him with a small smile, and followed the maid up the gray-laced marble stairs, with the footmen in tow just behind. They seemed to climb forever and Gwen wondered if she might actually be able to touch the angels overhead. When they reached her chambers, Gwen could see that Robert was right.

It was far more beautiful than she had expected. The elegant paper-hangings that covered every wall seemed new, and in the most recent Neo-Grecian fashion. From chair rail to cornice, the walls glowed with what appeared to be silk. The blankets and pillows on the bed looked as soft as clouds, and Gwen had to resist the urge to run her hands over them as the footmen deposited her luggage. High windows looked out upon a garden, though winter had left only green hedges and borders. A large dresser and armoire dominated the wall opposite the window and both gleamed with fresh polish. A charming dressing table, complete with oval mirror, sat in the corner.

It would certainly do.

Indeed, though she would be loathe to

admit it in anyone's presence, these chambers were infinitely more opulent than what she had at home. Some days in the Archer household there had not been enough firewood to keep the place warm, nor enough blanket layers to keep out the cold. Hard times had fallen upon her parents in recent years, and it would seem that their burdens would not lighten any time soon, now that Regina had vanished in the wind.

"Thank you, Frances," Gwen murmured absently. "I won't require any assistance until shortly before dinner. I will expect to see you back at six o'clock."

"Yes, Miss," the girl said, as she curtsied and then hurried out after the men, shutting the door behind her.

Gwen preferred to see to her own things and started by unpacking her trunks. A she sorted her clothes into the various drawers and shelved her dresses in the armoire, her thoughts inevitably turned back to Robert.

His behavior had been so, well, correct, for lack of a better word. But even as she thought it, an explanation sprang to her mind. Was he acting out of pity?

It was true that her family was nearly penniless, particularly now that they'd spent the last of father's money on a wedding that would not happen. Gwen had no prospects for suitors, and she was nearly at that age that men would begin to wonder *why* she had no suitors. She sat down on the bed, worry washing over her, even as another explanation assailed her: perhaps she herself had changed.

Regina's disappearance had not just thrown all their futures into confusion, it had made Gwen see people differently. She'd known her sister so well—or at least she'd thought she had. Now she found herself questioning everyone's motives for even the smallest thing. Was she also finding the worst in people as well?

She flopped back on the soft bed as her thoughts continued to whirl. Why hadn't Regina told her of her troubles? What could have been so pressing that she hadn't come to Gwen first? Indeed, her sister could have gone to their parents. Gwen closed her suddenly burning eyes. Her mother and father had been as wounded as she had been, if not more. Regina would have much to answer for when...

There was a knock at the door. "Miss?" said a small voice. "It's six o'clock."

## CHAPTER 2

*G*wen shook her head, trying to wake as she sat up. She'd fallen into such a deep sleep.

"Miss?" Frances said again. "Are you there?"

"Yes, Frances," Gwen said, slumber still in her voice. "Come in."

The exhaustion of worry, the burden of her sisterly duty, and the winter travel had all taken their toll.

Frances entered, curtsied, and closed the door behind her, before proceeding to light the candle on the nightstand.

Although Gwen wasn't used to having a lady's maid, she was immediately grateful. Frances helped her up from the bed. The girl was younger than she was, perhaps even younger than her sister, and considerably younger than the one servant that the Archers still employed—Alice, her old nurse. As their fortunes had sunk lower in these last few unkind years, her father had been forced to let the other servants go. But they could no sooner let Alice go than they could a member of the family. Ofttimes, it was Gwen or her mother who took care of Alice.

As Frances helped her change out of her dress, Gwen's thoughts returned to the present.

"I think I shall wear the periwinkle," she said, reaching for it from the armoire.

"Allow me, Miss," Frances said, removing it for her.

For just the briefest moment, the young girl ran her fingers over the shiny and almost sheer material of the long sleeve. Then she lifted it over Gwen's head and helped it to settle over her white petticoat and stays. When Frances finished with the row of buttons in the back, Gwen adjusted the neckline and sat at the dressing table.

By the way Frances deftly combed the stray locks of her hair into place and adjusted the hairpins, Gwen knew she must have experience, despite her youth.

"How long has Mr. Sheraton been at the hall?" Gwen asked of the maid's reflection.

Frances hesitated for a moment. "A week, Miss," she said. "The master wanted to make sure the hall was ready." The maid's lower lip trembled, but she said no more as she finished her task.

"That will be all, Frances," Gwen said, and watched the girl curtsy and leave.

Gwen leaned toward the mirror and examined her appearance critically. Her short slumber had done her some good. The dark circles under her eyes had almost gone, though not completely. Her skin, however, was pallid, which would not do. As she rose and stepped to the door, she pinched her cheeks.

Outside Gwen was met by another young lady that she didn't recognize.

She curtsied perfectly with a bow of her head. "Good evening, Miss," she said. "I'm Agnes. The master sent me to show you downstairs."

"I'm sure I'm grateful, Agnes," Gwen replied, smiling.

As Gwen followed the maid, she noticed that Agnes walked with a slight limp and also clasped the handrail. But her injury or infirmity, whichever it might be, did nothing to slow her descent. In only a few minutes, they were at the entrance hall, then the reception hall. At its end, a pair of footmen bowed to her and took hold of concealed handles behind them. What seemed to be a wall opened outward. Gwen nearly jumped back, and only managed to conceal her astonishment in time. She had arrived at the dining room.

Robert stood abruptly, almost knocking over his chair. He bowed awkwardly, not meeting her gaze, as she stifled a laugh. In a flash he was at her chair pulling it out for her. Smoothly, she took her seat, and watched as he returned to his.

All around them were panels of dark wood painted with tall, narrow murals, framed by inlaid mosaics. Each painting depicted scenes from antiquity, with temples that appeared to be home to the likes of Herakles, Theseus, and Pandora.

"It's not particularly to my taste," Robert

said. "But I haven't the heart to destroy the idyllic Greek countryside."

She hadn't been aware that he'd been watching her. "I certainly agree," she said.

He gestured to the footmen, who left and returned almost immediately with the soup.

"It is a pleasure to dine with you, Miss Archer," Robert said, as he tucked a strand of hair behind his ear. She recalled the same gesture from her arrival, and wondered if it might be a nervous habit. What would make a man like Robert nervous?

"Thank you for your hospitality, Mr. Sheraton," she replied.

As the soup was served, she stole a few glances at him, and noticed him doing the same.

"I trust your chambers are to your liking?" he inquired.

"Oh very much so," she said genuinely, before tasting the soup, though she could smell it. "Artichoke. One of my favorites." She took a spoonful. "This is delicious."

They ate their first course without any real conversation which gave Gwen time to try and absorb her surroundings. Like everything else at Dredthorne, she was starting to realize, the dining room with the doors that looked like walls was not what it seemed. However, she was aware that Robert was watching her over his glass of wine. Perhaps he had become a man of few words, not that he had ever talked that much. Or perhaps he was not a skilled conversationalist.

But then Gwen understood what might be keeping his tongue still. Naturally he was curious as to the nature of her news, and she hadn't spoken a word of it.

"I apologize that Regina isn't with me."

Robert examined her before setting down his spoon. "No such apologies are needed. In fact, if I can apologize for prying, I must ask you what happened. Your note was rather vague."

Gwen steadied herself, sitting up straight in her chair. Visions ran through her head of how badly he might react, and of the many ways this evening might end in disaster. She took a deep breath. There was no help for it but to begin.

"Regina has run away," she said slowly.

"She wrote a letter stating that she had lost herself, and has gone to find herself again."

Robert had enough grace to look surprised, even saddened, instead of enraged.

"It's nonsense, I know," she said apologetically. "But there were no warning signs, no strange habits that in retrospect could provide a clue as to what happened to change her mind. I feel terrible that I am going to have to break your poor brother's heart."

"Oh, Christopher couldn't possibly count that as your fault," he said. "Regina is but a child; so is Christopher, truly, but I know that my family was hoping that they could tame each other's impulses." He sighed as he shook his head. "It would have been such a good match."

Gwen was shocked; it was almost as if the old Robert had been replaced by a better mannered twin. In fact his wistful tone almost made it seem as though he were lamenting his own lack of a worthy match.

Or perhaps, Gwen thought, that was

what she wished to hear, due to her own very notable lack of suitors.

"I don't know where she could have gone," she finally confessed. "Or why she would have gone. If I had been in her place, awaiting my wedding..."

As the sentence died in her throat, Robert lowered his gaze, looking at the gleaming wood of the table intently as the main course was served. His face looked sorrowful as they ate the savory beef stew in companionable silence. She wondered what it was that he had gone through that had taught him some manners. He had not even raised his voice when she had told him the news.

"We have a had a mild winter," he finally ventured. "I daresay the gardener is glad of it."

"Do you grow your own artichokes?" she asked.

Their conversation ranged across a hundred little nothings, as though by some secret agreement they avoided the topic that had brought her to the hall. They talked about the upkeep of the mansion and the renovations that had been done to her room. Gwen was most interested in the discussion of the grounds and why they had been built so very far away from anyone else. The hall was so remote that she couldn't think of any reason why the original settlers would have built here at all.

After their dessert course, Robert stood, helping Gwen from her chair. "I may not have all of the answers to Dredthorne's mysteries, but I may have some clue where to find them. Would you like to see the hidden library?"

Gwen's attention peaked. "A hidden library? Truly?"

She had always loved books. There had never been enough in her father's library to sate her curiosity. Gwen had always wanted to know more, to know the answers *why*. Her father had said it was a curse in a woman to ask such questions, but her mother had called it wisdom whenever Father was out of earshot.

Robert went to the Pandora panel painting and pressed a finger to the portrait. Gwen went still as something clicked and the painting swung open.

"Why, that is a door," she exclaimed.

Beyond the painting lay a large space that smelled of dust and old books, a scent that Gwen found positively intriguing. Inside, it was obvious that Robert hadn't been the first one to discover it; unlike the hall itself, the books were meticulously cared for, dusted, and organized. She ran her fingers across the covers of several on a low, polished table, frowning.

"What are these?" she said.

They were smaller than the rest, and thinner. Fine leather bound the antique pages, and they were in remarkable repair.

Robert had gone to the opposite wall, and was perusing what appeared to be an antique Bible.

"Pardon? Oh. Those are a collection of journals from Mr. Thorne's wife, Beatrice Thorne."

"The builder of the hall?" she asked.

When Robert nodded, Gwen sat down at the table, pulling the first journal toward her. What would it have been like to be married to the man who had created such a bizarre estate? Two of the pages were stuck together, and she carefully peeled them apart. The handwriting was impeccable; if only her own penmanship was half as beautiful as this woman's measured script.

*DEAR JOURNAL –*

*Today I arrived at Dredthorne Hall. Mr. Thorne has created such a beautiful home for us; I have never been so excited in all of my time to see what our lives will bring us together. I know of no other land that is as welcoming and exotic as the hall's grounds.*

*We left from our honeymoon at the seaside and traveled to the hall at speed. The carriage bounded lightly against the road, and Mr. Thorne and I held hands every moment of the way, enjoying each other's company.*

*As we approached, I admired the dark shutters that hugged each brightly shining window. The bright red door was intensely welcoming, and there was a small shadow in the window of the attic.*

"SHE'S RUMORED to have been cursed, you know," Robert said quietly.

Gwen could feel his eyes upon her as

she flipped through the journal's pages but she couldn't look away. It seemed like such a promising start to a marriage. Finally, though, Robert's words sank in.

Gwen paused with her fingertips over the neat writing. "I beg your pardon?" Certainly she had heard him incorrectly, for Robert was not prone to jesting.

He sat down at the table across from her, causing the small chair to creak. Clearly, the books took precedence in terms of upkeep.

"There's a legend in the village of Renwick that every owner of Dredthorne Hall is cursed," he said, laying the Bible down on the table. "Every master of Dredthorne is doomed to fall in love with a lady who has stayed overnight at the hall; and she will die, no matter how strong his love, before their first wedding anniversary."

She flicked back through the pages, noting that the journals began when Mr. Thorne had begun courting Beatrice, the future Mrs. Thorne. They were the work of a young woman, these pages of precise script. Could she possibly have not been healthy?

Gwen stopped her line of thought when she realized what she'd done: given credence to a musty old legend. She sat back and leveled a steady gaze at Robert. "Before the first anniversary, you say?" Though she'd tried to keep her voice neutral, she hadn't succeeded.

Robert shook his head, smiling slightly. "I know that you don't believe me, but it's quite true, Miss Archer. Each woman since Mrs. Thorne has gone mad or died." He shrugged, and got up, taking the Bible back to its shelf. "Perhaps the journals will illuminate the dark and inscrutable past of the hall."

Her fingers paused over the pages. Did she really want to know if such a thing could possibly be true? But before long, she was reading in full, the hidden library fallen away.

ROBERT WATCHED Gwen for a long moment as she delved into the journal of Beatrice

Thorne. Though he hadn't read it, she was clearly fascinated, and something about her interest and intensity charmed him. He took a deep breath and wished, not for the first time, that Christopher would soon arrive. For there had never been a day, from the moment that he had met Gwen, that he had not been in love with her.

Even now she beguiled him, from the simple way she held the journal so carefully to the way she smiled as she turned the pages. From the minute he'd mentioned the library, there'd been a certain, very lovely light in her sea green eyes. It was going to be hell to wake in the same place as her, knowing that they were so close—and yet apart.

There had always been many things about Gwen that he admired: her honesty and steadfast nature; her obvious devotion to family. But it was her beauty, in such close proximity, that now entranced him. Her brunette curls framed a heart-shaped face whose skin was so perfect that it could belong to a newborn. He wondered what it would be like to reach out and touch it.

He cleared his throat and sat back in his

chair. He was musing on nonsense. Nothing of the sort could happen now that Christopher had been accepted by Regina.

Gwen's mouth had opened slightly, mouthing the words she read, and her face had gone pale.

"What are you reading?" he asked.

"There's a letter tucked in this diary," she said, and her hand shook as she lifted the page out of the journal. "A letter from a Miss Louisa Wilson."

Robert frowned, tilting his head as he brushed the hair back from his eyes. "I know that name. If I'm not mistaken, Miss Wilson was a courtesan," he said. "She disappeared here at Dredthorne, perhaps some fifty years ago."

Gwen's eyes blazed with interest. "*Did she.*" She scanned the letter again, looking up and down the page. "Here," she said, pointing to one passage in particular. "She believed someone was going to harm her."

"Strange," he said. "Who here would want to harm her?" He paused as he reflected. "Well, perhaps Mrs. Thorne, but I can't believe a woman of her background could do such a thing. Besides, Miss

Wilson was not murdered. She disappeared."

Gwen carefully folded the letter and put it back. "I think we need to find out what happened to her." She looked into his eyes. "I think if we can manage that, we'll unlock more mystery than just that."

Did her soft voice carry a hint of worry? Though he'd only suggested that she look at the library as a bit of a diversion, she'd obviously become quite interested.

"Perhaps bring the journals with you," he suggested. "I'll help you to carry them. We can study them while we wait for Christoper."

Gwen stared at the long row of journals and quickly began to make a pile of certain ones. As they gathered up the small mountain of books, Robert wondered what he had just gotten himself into.

# CHAPTER 3

*O*ver the next few days as they waited for Christopher, Robert noted that life at Dredthorne Hall had settled implausibly into a routine of sorts. After breakfast, he and Gwen roamed the hall together, exploring distant staircases, looking for more secret rooms, and hunting for evidence of long forgotten foul play. They'd discovered a music room and even a medical supply closet, but nothing that shed any light on the fate of Miss Wilson. After lunch, Gwen would retire to read through the journals while Robert managed his affairs, as he did now.

He sighed, closing his eyes at the mountain of work before him. His father would have delighted in it—if he'd been here. The man took to paperwork like slaying a dragon. But increasingly, it was Robert's duty to conquer the letters, records, and every other document pertaining to the household. His father's health was in steep decline. They'd sent for the best doctors, healers, and medicines—everything that he and his mother could possibly think of, and more. But there seemed no solution to his increasingly watery cough and the swelling around his too thin waist.

Robert had to face up to the fact that he would soon be the head of the household—and he wasn't sure how he would accomplish it. His mother was a wonderful wife to the elder Sheraton, and admirably managed their home in London. But Robert had no such help, nor any prospects for such.

His valet, Parks, appeared at the door. "May I help you prepare for dinner, sir?"

Dinner? How long had he been staring daggers at the onerous pile of papers. "Certainly, Parks."

James Parks had served the Sheraton family for nearly thirty years, as had his father William before him. Always immaculate, he kept his gray and receding hairline oiled and combed back, his black suit clean and pressed, and his tie precisely knotted.

As Parks dressed him, Robert forced his thoughts away from London and back to Dredthorne. Why were women going missing at the hall? Nothing that he and Gwen had seen, aside from the journals, had given any indication.

As he walked down to dinner, he met her at the bottom of the stairs. Her sea green gown was the perfect complement to her jewel-like eyes. When he offered his arm, she smiled radiantly and graciously accepted it. He escorted her into the dining room and then to her seat, before motioning for the first course. But when he took his place and saw the onion soup, he almost pushed it away. He looked up to see Gwen watching him, a smirk curling the corner of her mouth.

"You as well?" she asked.

"Definitely," he said, moving the bowl aside. "I'd rather eat a salad like a rabbit than taste one spoonful of onion soup." He motioned for the next course. "What have you found in the journals?"

"Mrs. Thorne was definitely jealous of the courtesan," she began eagerly. "She was famous for her many, shall we say, talents. She danced beautifully, and Mrs. Thorne couldn't dance at all."

He listened to her rush on, smiling as she spoke. In fact, he barely noticed the servants taking away the abysmal soup. But as she described how Miss Wilson played cards and was even known to gamble with the men, a tiny piece of white plaster landed on the table between them.

He gazed up as Gwen asked, "What is that?"

But Robert had no time to answer as he flew from his seat, dashed to where she sat, and shoved her out of the way. The massive chandelier crashed onto the table a second later, shattering the wood and sending splinters in every direction. He dove to the ground and covered her with his body as she cried out. For several moments there was no sound at all, then the servants began shouting.

Robert pushed himself up enough to see Gwen's face. "Are you all right?"

Tears brimmed in her eyes, but she nodded a vigorous yes. Slowly he helped her to sit up and they surveyed the damage. The footmen were hurriedly putting out the many candles that had fallen, and it appeared that nothing had burnt. But the chandelier's crystals were scattered in every direction, and the thick iron of its central support had driven into the table like a harpoon. Large splinters of wood were impaled in the back of Gwen's chair. Robert realized that she had come very close to being seriously injured.

As the servants fluttered around them, Robert helped her to stand.

"*Heavens,*" Gwen muttered, putting a hand to her heart as she stared at the devastation. "We could have been…"

Robert blocked her view of the chair and motioned to Frances. "Escort Miss Archer to her chambers," he told the young woman, her staring eyes as big as saucers. "Frances," he said sharply, and she finally blinked.

"Yes, master," she said, with a quick bob.

"You'll stay with her until I say so," he ordered.

"Yes, sir," she answered.

"Robert..." Gwen reached out for him, her hand trembling.

He gently took it with both of his. "You need to lie down, Gwen. Please, you've had a shock. Let Frances help you." He looked over to Agnes. "Fetch a glass of brandy for Miss Archer and take it to her room." Both maids curtsied and he reluctantly let go of Gwen's hand. With a final long look at him, she nodded and followed the two women from the room.

Despite feeling like he could use a brandy himself, Robert took charge of the clean up. The servants, obviously unnerved, set to their tasks nevertheless. As they did, he looked up at the ceiling.

Four ragged holes in the panels surrounded an even larger one in the middle. Had all of them come loose at once? Or had one come undone, taking the others with it? Though Robert had never hung a chandelier in his life, he found it unlikely that such a monumental piece of lighting would be secured by anything but the strongest of means. Nor had there been the slightest indication that a failure of its securing mechanism was imminent. He had dined here every night since he'd arrived.

If not for that small piece of plaster…

Tomorrow he would bring a ladder to investigate, when there was more light. But even now he suspected that another Dredthorne mystery might be in the making.

"We hardly need another," he muttered.

"Sir?" Parks said.

His valet stood in front of him with a brush in one hand and a pan filled with crystals in the other. "Nothing, Parks." He looked around the dining room, which had almost been cleared. "When you're finished with that, find your bed. We won't be having dinner. Tell the others as well, if you would." He glanced up at the ceiling again. "I'll be inspecting that in the morning."

"Very good, sir," Parks said, glancing upward as well.

As Robert climbed the stairs he realized that his hands were in fists. In fact, he clenched them so hard that the skin of his knuckles stretched tight. A heated rage had been building inside him ever since he'd had to push Gwen to the floor. As he passed her door, he paused, listening, wanting nothing more than to go to her this instant and quell her fears. But the room was quiet and he hoped that the brandy had worked its good effect.

As he turned away, he resolved to order the servants to check every bolt and screw of every room he'd planned on using. He was going to keep Gwen safe, so that she would never fear again.

* * *

As THE DAYS PASSED, Gwen found that the fright of the chandelier had gone, probably due to Robert's efforts to assure himself that all else was safe. But it was also growing obvious to her that Christopher was not coming to Dredthorne Hall. His silence was compounded by the complete lack of any message from Regina, and Gwen was ready to give up on ever finding her poor missing sister. Clearly, the young woman did not want to be found and had made every effort to keep her family from knowing where she had gone. Where she had learned such stealthy skills, Gwen could not imagine.

In the week since she had arrived, Robert had turned some of the running of the household over to her. Though she suspected it was to keep her mind occupied, she relished the challenge. The day after the incident with the crashing chandelier, when Robert had ordered the servants to pore over the house for any other such issues, she had supervised them and noted a few lanterns that were in need of service or repair. However the rest of the house was fairly sound, if rather in need of a revitalizing uplift. Gwen began to divert some of the servants from their normal tasks to the upkeep of the rooms they were using; cleaning, of course, and some moderate repair. She also oversaw the restoration of broken doors and torn paper-hangings and made note of rooms where the damage was so profound that new wall coverings would be needed. Gwen was a little surprised that she was actually good at organizing.

Instead of their usual long walks around

the grounds, Robert had taken the mornings to discover what had happened to his brother. He had started by writing feverish letters to his parents, to London, to an address Christopher had once stayed at it in Paris, and to anyone who may have heard from him—but there was no trace of where Christopher had gone. No one had seen him, at least no one who would admit it to the elder Sheraton brother.

At about the same time, Gwen had begun to use her spare time to organize notes from the journals in the library. She could at least attempt to trace a narrative trail of the courtesan who had gone missing. In the evenings, over dinner she would relate all of her latest findings.

But what she never mentioned, for fear that it would make her seem silly, was that, when the house was quiet, she sometimes thought she heard a woman crying. Her dressing room could become eerily silent, without even the sound of the wind. It was at those precise moments that the temperature would feel as if it were dipping a little, though she couldn't be certain that it wasn't her imagination. Then a low, barely audible moan seemed to emanate from nowhere, followed by the muffled sound of sobbing, but never long enough for her to trace.

To complement her hours of ghost hunting through the books in the library, Gwen spent her afternoons physically scouring the hall, looking for the source of the sounds, but to no avail.

Likewise her hunt for hidden doors and mysteries, hoping to find a hint of what had happened to the vanished Miss Wilson, regularly ended in disappointment. A courtesan of such fame and notoriety should not have just gone missing; it should have been a scandal, something noteworthy, but she had found nothing to indicate that anyone at all had noticed. The expeditions throughout the old hall had not uncovered any more than her work in the library had—and today was no exception.

As she climbed the stairs and entered her chamber, Gwen was once again forced to admit defeat. She sat down on her bed, discouraged, and tossed her notes onto the desk. As usual at such moments, her thoughts turned to Robert. He'd become more and more protective of her since the chandelier incident. It was almost as if he'd come to feel responsible for her. Or perhaps even deeper emotions were at play.

She waved a hand in the air. "What nonsense."

He'd certainly made no such declaration, despite there being ample opportunity. She stood up as if that act alone would stop her wild speculation. When it didn't she decided to select her dinner dress, even though it was early.

But as she approached the dressing room and the late afternoon light spilled in, she saw an imperfection in the floor, where it abutted the wall. Though the inspection of the house that she'd done with the servants wouldn't have revealed so small a thing, perhaps it was worth taking note.

She frowned as she drew closer. The imperfection wasn't only in the floor; it travelled up the wall. In fact, a thin, crumbling line of plaster appeared when she moved aside the small chair. Now she could see that the faint crack ran from the floor up to the very ceiling. This was more than a small imperfection.

As she'd seen the men do during their examinations, she rapped the wall next to the crack, dislodging a billow of dust. Waving her hand in front of her face, she retreated for a moment and let the particles settle. When she returned, a closer inspection revealed a seam of some sort— and it had to be intentional. It was perfectly straight and fractionally wider now. Using her fists and braving the fine powder that rained down, she quickly discovered a second seam, parallel to the first and about a yard away. As she stood with hands on hips staring at the two lines, a thought occurred to her. With both hands on the walls and her feet firmly planted, she gave the wall a shove. To her astonishment, it moved inward at one seam, and outward at the other.

"A revolving door," she whispered. "A hidden one." Or formerly hidden.

But beyond its dusty threshold was only pure darkness.

She raced to her nightstand, lit the candle, and brought it back. There, at the limit of its light, was a low passage. The tunnel was about half her height so Gwen was forced to kneel down. With the candle in front of her, she slowly crawled forward. For what felt like an eternity, she made her way through more dust and the occasional cob web. But there was no option but to press forward unless she wanted to back out, since there wasn't enough room left to turn around. As she began to worry, thinking that she would at any moment be led to a dead end, the passage dropped out in front of her.

Her eyes and the candle light settled on the stone steps of a stairway. She gasped in delight and held the small flame higher. Maybe this passage would hold the answers to her questions about Miss Wilson.

Carefully she slid down the first steps until she could stand. Still proceeding cautiously, she descended the stairs, traveling to what had to be the first floor, only to find a wall that barred her way.

But was it really a wall, she wondered, lifting her candle to it. This time the seams in the plaster were obvious. Using her shoulder, she pushed the revolving door, but only a little. There was no telling what or who might be on the other side.

The door creaked softly from long disuse, and almost immediately the scent of dinner wafted through the crack and crept into her nostrils. Gwen frowned. Why was there a secret passage, long abandoned, from her dressing room to the kitchen? Why would someone possibly want to go into the kitchen in secret, other than a late night snack, without the servants realizing it?

The bustle and clatter of this evening's dinner preparations must have covered any noises that Gwen had made because no one gave any sign of noticing. She peered out into the cook's kitchen through the crack. She must be between the ice chest and a thick wooden counter. There was a small table immediately in front of the door, and it seemed to be the pie preparation station.

This passageway made no sense on its own, but perhaps it somehow related to all the other secrets of Dredthorne Hall. She closed the revolving door.

The next mystery for her to solve was how long it would take for her to crawl back up to her room. When she finally emerged several minutes later with dust and dirt covering her in a fine layer, she sneezed repeatedly, shaking her head. Though she was no closer to finding out what had happened to the courtesan, she was thrilled with her discovery. But now it truly was time to get ready for the evening's dinner. This passage hadn't given her any real secrets, she was fairly certain of that. But it meant that there might be other mysteries in the hall, other passageways that might lead to places that even Robert had not yet discovered. And one of those expeditions might lead her to the answers regarding the mystery that was plaguing her: the disappearance of the courtesan.

When Frances arrived, she said nothing at the state of her clothing; she did, however, tsk over Gwen's abused hair.

"I must wash this with a wet cloth, Miss," she said timidly. "Nothing saving it but a do over."

Although Frances glanced at her filthy clothes more than once, Gwen said nothing, not willing to give up her secrets to anyone but Robert.

"Frances," she said suddenly.

"Yes, Miss?" Frances was biting her lip over the process of drying and pinning Gwen's hair, concentrating hard on making each tendril perfect.

"Have you heard any noises?" Gwen asked neutrally. It wouldn't do for the servants to start wondering if she'd gone insane.

"Noises, Miss?" She ran the comb through an errant curl in Gwen's hair, frowning as the strand refused to comply. "I'm not certain I take the mistress's meaning."

Gwen noted that Frances refused to meet her eye, and pressed on, wondering if there was something that the maid was keeping from her.

"I've been hearing this...crying. It's almost not audible at all but I believe I can make out the sounds of a moan and perhaps sobbing. It's muffled, as if coming from a great distance." She paused, watching Frances in the mirror. "Have you heard it?"

Frances stayed silent for a long time, but then said, "There are rumors, Miss."

Her fingers put the finishing touches on Gwen's hair.

"Rumors?" Gwen prompted.

"Rumors about the ghosts, Miss, rumors about the hauntings, the Thornes, the hall…" She shrugged. "There are things that happen here that can't be explained."

Gwen decided to let the topic drop as Frances helped her into her evening dress. Nor did Frances utter another word. With the buttons at her back fastened, Gwen dismissed the young maid, and thought perhaps there was a bit more quickness in her departure.

That suited Gwen, since she was in a hurry herself. There was so much to tell Robert, and she knew that she had to remain hopeful that he might have something to tell her about Christopher. It was still possible that Christopher was simply delayed and that there might be word from him soon.

But even as she thought it, she knew it was wishful thinking, because she was not sure how much longer she could be in the same hall with Robert without confessing her fears—and her growing infatuation with the man she had once regarded as contemptuous.

But before she departed, in the pervading silence, Gwen listened carefully. *There it was again*—the distant crying. She could hear it only from the corner of her chambers near the dressing room. She had been over and over the nearby rooms, and now a secret passage, but she'd never found anything that would indicate the source of the crying. It was growing less frequent, as if the woman it belonged to was exhausted beyond measure. Then, as mysteriously as it had begun, it stopped. Though Gwen listened intently, nothing more came.

"Who are you?" she whispered. "*Where* are you?"

Was this one of the ghosts of Dredthorne Hall? Was it their aim to drive her mad? The curse could not possibly settle upon her if Robert was not the official owner of the hall, surely. Nor did she count as a woman staying overnight, one that would be killed before her first wedding anniversary. Certainly there could be no anniversary without a wedding. Yes, that was it. Even if there was a curse, it simply did not apply to her.

And ghosts? She'd been frightened by the chandelier incident, and many of the servants had been too. Since there'd been no evidence of sabotage, the old rumors of hauntings naturally surfaced. Yes, that would explain it.

She felt better, or at least she told herself that she did, and hurried downstairs to the makeshift dining room they'd set up in one of the living rooms. She found Robert waiting, a pleasant smile on his lips, as he held her chair for her. As she took her seat, she noticed that they were having salad rather than soup. She grinned at Robert as he sat down.

"The kitchen staff do take suggestions, you know," he said. "So what have your explorations given us to talk about this evening?"

Though she'd wanted to draw out the tale and tease him with the ending, her excitement got the better of her.

"Actually I found a hidden passage in my dressing room. Behind a revolving door. It was quite dusty and full of cobwebs."

He smiled a little. "Walking through a dusty passage with cobwebs, Gwen?" he said, chuckling. "Next time try something more plausible."

"Actually, I was crawling," she said, looking directly into his dark eyes. "It was even worse than all that. But I eventually came to find that it ends in the cook's kitchen."

He frowned. "You're serious." She nodded eagerly. "The cook's kitchen? How strange. It would be shorter to go down the stairs if you truly needed to go to the kitchen." He glanced in that direction, craning his neck. "Perhaps we should–"

There was a loud crack and Gwen give a little shriek, as Robert disappeared.

"Robert!" she cried, standing so quickly that she knocked her chair back. But as soon as she rounded the table, she found him. He was sprawled on the floor, his head not an inch from the stone hearth behind him.

"What in the name of…" he muttered as he got to his feet.

One of the footmen ran over to them. "Sir, have you been harmed?"

Robert dusted off his coat. "Not at all. It was just a little accident. You can see to the dinner." Though the man looked worried, he bowed before retreating.

Robert knelt beside the wooden chair, examining it carefully, and frowned. "The back legs of the chair have snapped."

"You could have been killed," Gwen declared. She could see it all now in her mind's eye—the blood spattered against the hearth, his head dashed open against the stone. Shuddering, she put a hand to her mouth.

He stood and took her hand, patting it gently. His hand was so warm, and she found that she relaxed instantly at its touch.

"I'm fine, Gwen," he said softly. "I promise. Just bruised pride and a small reminder of my mortality." He turned to one of the serving maids. "Fetch Parks, please."

His valet reported immediately and looked horrified. "Sir, what happened?" He rushed to Robert's side, kneeling down to examine the chair.

"It looks," Robert said and hesitated, glancing at Gwen. "It looks as though the wood has been sawed through. Do you have any explanation for this?"

Gwen felt herself go pale, but stood up straight as she waited for Parks' answer.

"No, sir," he replied gravely. "I'll question the other servants to see if anyone has seen anything strange."

Gwen's hand began to shake and Robert held it tighter.

"Good," he replied. As Parks picked up the chair and was about to leave, Robert stopped him. "Check the rest of the chairs as well."

"Very good, sir," he said, and bowed before leaving.

"Robert?" Gwen heard herself whisper.

"Yes, Gwen?"

"What did you say about this hall being haunted?"

# CHAPTER 4

On the following day, Parks was able to report that all of the chairs at Dredthorne had been inspected. None showed any signs of tampering, damage, or rot. Though Robert should have been glad at the news, he was infuriated. He'd searched the secret passage that Gwen had discovered, and found nothing except for the passage itself. Looking at the ceiling where the chandelier had once hung also revealed nothing. His stream of letters and inquiries regarding Christopher and his whereabouts had amounted to nothing. All of his efforts resulted in nothing.

This morning was yet another frustrating example.

"Damn it," Robert cursed softly.

He rested his forehead on his hands, staring down at the mountain of paperwork. As his father's health continued to decline, he was left with managing the family's investments, as well as the investigation into Christopher's disappearance. But it was the situation at Dredthorne that consumed him. Something was amiss in the old house, and Gwen was on to something with this hidden passage of hers; he was sure of it. But where was the connection? What did chandeliers and chairs have to do with hidden doorways, secret libraries, and concealed corridors? Every day there were more questions, and not a single answer. In another week, he'd be hunting ghosts.

He checked his watch and was relieved. It was time to find Gwen for their daily stroll in the gardens. He looked forward to these walks more than he wanted to admit.

Downstairs he found her at the back of the house, as usual. Though she wore her coat, it fitted her figure to perfection. She smiled when she saw him, her delicate features radiant. Though she'd obviously recovered from the fright of the previous evening, he somehow wished she hadn't. He'd enjoyed holding her hand and simply having her near.

"You are quite beautiful, Miss Archer," he found himself saying, then inwardly winced.

What had come over him? She'd allowed him to hold her hand—for just the briefest of moments—not pledge her undying love. In truth, he had no inkling of her thoughts toward him for she had never expressed any. And yet the way her features had paled when she'd thought him injured... Perhaps he had read too much into that.

But as he warred with himself, Gwen simply smiled. "Thank you, Mr. Sheraton," she said warmly, and took his arm. They made their way toward the glass doors, and exited into the garden. "How has your work been today?"

Robert groaned at the question. "Well, my brother has fallen off of the earth. No one seems to know where he is, and truthfully, I am about to write home and declare that he is missing."

He'd only delayed this long because of

the consequences that he felt would surely come. His mother would have an apoplexy and his father's fading health would not be able to withstand such news. In short, he could become both an orphan and a man whose only brother had vanished.

"I'm so sorry," Gwen replied softly, and in her voice Robert heard true sorrow.

As she squeezed his arm, he considered declaring his feelings for her. But the same old obstacle presented itself: his brother had declared himself for her sister, who had accepted him. Until that matter was resolved, there was nothing Robert could do.

They walked through the tall shrubbery and past the kitchen garden in silence as they approached Gwen's favorite place on their circuit, the mossy pond. The overwintering Mallards there liked to talk back to them as she and Robert chatted on the stone bench. They took their seat but had neglected to bring their little friends the usual bread crumbs. Instead, both they and the ducks sat quietly among the brilliantly yellow witch hazel and the delicate pink blooms of elephant's ears.

Robert exhaled slowly. "I'm worried about writing to my parents about Christopher," he confessed.

Gwen's delicate fingers threaded through his, and he made no move to dislodge them. "When I read Regina's letter, I thought the world was going to end. My mother cried for days, while my father said nothing. It was frightening and I thought they'd both come undone. Worry absolutely consumed me." She patted his arm. "But then, after about a week, at dinner, my father looked at my mother and simply said, 'I never liked Christopher anyway.'"

Robert blinked and stared at her. Only when she could no longer suppress her smile and started to giggle did he begin to laugh as well. Gods it felt good simply to sit and laugh. "You are incorrigible my dear Miss Archer," he said, still chuckling. "I am sure that your father said no such thing."

"Ah, but that is what makes my tale all the more entertaining," she assured him. "For he did in fact say it."

Now Robert had to frown. "Surely not. I

can't imagine such a thing. Your parents adore Christopher."

Her smiling eyes met his. "Well the point *wasn't* that he didn't like Christopher. The point was that even when things were looking to be at their worst, my family rallied together. I just know that no matter what has become of Christopher, your mother and father will support you in your search and your efforts."

"That may be true," Robert said, the levity now vanished. "But I am afraid that my father may not be able to support anyone for very much longer."

"Oh, no," she breathed, gazing up at him from under a furrowed brow. "Your father?"

Robert nodded. "The doctors have told my mother to prepare herself," he said quietly, then shook his head. "How can one truly prepare oneself for such an eventuality?"

To that Gwen had no answer, though he hadn't expected one.

The ducks must have become bored or hungry, since they waddled off and splashed into the pond, their orange feet paddling beneath the water. With the coming change of the seasons, they would be off, flying back to the colder climate from which they had come to take shelter here. He cocked his head at them as they swam together, leaving little wakes behind them. It was odd to think of anyone, even ducks, taking shelter at Dredthorne.

"I do know what you mean," Gwen finally said. "How does one prepare for the inexplicable? For some reason that I cannot fathom, I do not think Regina is going to come back. Perhaps it is an intuition, or perhaps I just despair, but something inside me says that she will not return."

"She may not return to Renwick," he said, "but I'm sure she'll turn up." He squeezed her hand. "She has a wonderful sister like you to take care of her, and parents who love her. Why wouldn't she want to come back to that?" He paused for a moment, watching the ducks dive for their food. "I can see why she might not want to come back to Christopher, though. The man snores like a saw cutting wood." He cleared his throat. "No doubt your father heard him."

Gwen giggled a bit, a sound that Robert found delightful. As usual, their garden walk had done him a world of good. Sunlight glittered on the surface of the mossy pond like wavy emeralds; the chill of the morning was lifting; and Dredthorne didn't seem quite as imposing, nor his troubles so pressing, as they did just an hour ago.

IN THE BACK of the kitchen, the servants sat at the wooden table that kept them far from the ears of the master and mistress. As usual, the mysteries of Dredthorne Hall were the topic of animated conversation. Parks sat listening as Agnes, Jonathan, and Frances gossiped over their tea and biscuits.

"And I say," Agnes continued, "that this ghost business is nonsense. My parents worked here and my great uncle and none of them ever went mad or were struck deaf, dumb, or dead."

Jonathan shook his head. "I wouldn't be too sure about that. There ain't no spirits in the stables, but I have seen and heard enough things in this house to make me wonder. Stranger things in Earth and Heaven than... Well, you know what I mean."

"It's what I have been saying all along, isn' it," Frances said. "There are times on the upper floors when I hear the strangest sounds, like a sob, or a groan–"

"Or the wind," Parks put in. "Really, the lot of you. You sound like frightened school children."

"Well, it's not just us," Frances countered. "Miss Gwen hears something too sometimes. She gets that strange tilt of her head, like she is listening for something just beyond hearing. And..." Frances leaned forward and lowered her voice. "When I came to dress her for dinner the other day, she was covered in dust and cobwebs and dirt. I think the ghosts are leading her deeper into the hall." She looked at Parks. "Explain that one, Mr. Parks."

He scowled at her over his tea and finished sipping before he answered. "How many ways are there for a dress to get dirty, Frances? Really. Some of the rooms in the hall have barely been opened and cleaned. You see how she explores and supervises the repair work."

"It's all hogwash," Agnes agreed. "You're letting your imagination run away with you. I say there is nothing in this hall but a few loose fixtures and rat's nests. You'll see, once it's all fixed up."

"Exactly my point," Parks agreed. "We've just made a start. Why do you think we hear nothing here in the servant's rooms? Because we've made sure that everything here is ready and working."

Jonathan took one of the freshly baked biscuits and took a decisive bite as he stood. "Well, I've got to get back to the stables." But Parks heard him tack on under his breath, "Thank goodness."

"Well I say thank goodness that it's not the servants that have anything to fear from the curse on this hall," Frances said, watching him go. "It's the master's true love that is undone by its evil eye, someone he marries."

Agnes nodded. "That much is true." Then she winked at Frances. "I'm just glad Mr. Sheraton has never taken a fancy to me. Frances here would be more to his taste."

Frances choked a bit on her tea. "I wouldn't know anything about that."

"Never mind, Frances," Agnes said. "I'm only teasing. It's plain to see that the master only has eyes for his lady guest. If the hall is calling to her, showing her things, than I can only hope she never marries him no matter how much he dotes on her." A mischievous grin spread across her face. "In her younger days, she might have looked a bit like you. Better be careful if you start hearing things too."

As she sipped her tea, Frances sputtered and coughed.

Parks took out his pocket watch. "Enough idle chit chat. We must see to dinner."

## CHAPTER 5

*D*inner had been quiet and, thankfully, uneventful. Gwen had particularly enjoyed the Welsh rarebit and the grilled mackerel, as had Robert. Though at first she thought he'd only agreed to their garden walks and choice of foods in order to be agreeable, it seemed that they genuinely appreciated the same things. There'd been little new to report from either of them, so they'd played a brief game of piquet. Gwen had proved lucky in cards this evening, and Robert had seemed to bear his losses with equanimity. It had all been quite pleasant and normal.

Now she lay in bed under the pale moonlight, waiting for sleep to come. But as always, of late, her thoughts turned to

Robert. He'd confided to her in the garden today in a way that no other man had ever done. Rather than think him weak when he'd confessed worry for his parents, she found that it endeared him to her. They were alike in this way, in their devotion to family. Of all the things she expected to find at Dredthorne, surely that had not been one of them.

She blew out a breath. Sleep was obviously nowhere near. Her gaze fell on the journals that she and Robert had brought up. Perhaps they would distract her. She got up, put on her dressing gown, and lit a candle.

"What happened to you, Miss Wilson?" she said to no one.

Earlier, she'd found a letter from her, tucked between the pages of one of Mrs. Thorne's journals. Though it revealed little, she read it again, impressed once more by how rushed the handwriting seemed.

*My Darling,*

*I hope this finds you well. Spring has arrived in the countryside with a vengeance.*

*Wildflowers seem to bloom everywhere and the staff take pains to keep all the vases full, even the large Chinese urns in the entrance hall.*

*My stay in the great house has been rather pleasant until now. Mr. Thorne is an excellent host. I find I am entertained by his reading to me from his wonderful library in the evenings. He insists that he shall teach me to ride, so that I can accompany him in the mornings. The cook here is wonderful and my maid quite diligent.*

*But I fear that not all of the family or staff approve of my presence here under Dredthorne's roof. I have my own set of rooms, but I have seen Mrs. Thorne wandering the corridors when I return to my bedchamber in the early mornings. Of all things, one of the stable boys has been asking a great many questions about my past and my future.*

*There have been some accidents around the hall of late. I'm nervous that they may be brought on by more than just unfortunate circumstances. I fear that someone is going to*

GOING TO WHAT? Why had the letter not

been finished? Is that the moment that she had gone missing?

Gwen mused for a moment on the possibility that the courtesan's disappearance might be the fuel for the rumors of the hall being haunted. But reading the letter again had proved no more illuminating than the first time. She tucked it back into the journal and went back to bed.

Burrowing under the covers, she closed her eyes, trying not to think of whatever "unfortunate circumstance" might have befallen Miss Wilson. Instead, Gwen decided to think of weddings, particularly the one that she and her mother had planned for Regina and Christopher. They'd have made a handsome couple, but now she realized that Robert would easily have eclipsed his brother and made a very dashing best man.

"Heavens," she muttered. She was thinking of him again.

With an exasperated sigh, she turned onto her side. Unfortunately, staring at the window did little to distract her. Instead her mind turned from the courtesan, to

Mrs. Thorne, to her husband, to the Dredthorne curse, to Robert and Christopher, to Regina, and back again. Such thoughts continued to swirl through her head, until at last her eyelids grew heavy.

Someone crept into the room so softly that she barely heard them. With deft and fluid movements, they slid into the bed behind her, resting a hand on her hip.

"I could not help but to come see you," Robert said softly.

His fingertips gently caressed her side, and she shivered, feeling as though she were in that dim place between wakefulness and sleep. Dazed, she leaned her head back against the strength of his chest as he lightly slid his fingers across her waist, making her shudder against him. With a start, she realized that he was wearing nothing more than his sleeping clothes, not even a robe.

"Robert," she murmured, her eyes half-closed, as she reached back to hold his hand. He raised up and kissed the side of her neck lightly, then trailed his soft lips down her shoulder, and closed his teeth gently over her skin. Whimpering, she clutched his hand, and he slowly brought it up to her breast.

His hand cupped her flesh and his clever fingers plucked at her pebbling nipple. Her body responded to his touch as if it'd been born for the very purpose. As he slipped his other hand beneath her and pulled her close, warmth spread down her belly. As though he'd sensed it, his hand found its way beneath her nightgown and his fingers slipped between her legs.

"Yes," she whispered hoarsely. "*Yes.*"

"Shh," he murmured softly, his voice deep and husky. "Let me pleasure you. You have done so much for me, Gwen." Then he touched her, gathering the wetness from between her legs to rub against her throbbing nub. She squirmed against him, pressing back into him as she whimpered.

"*Robert,*" she breathed. What he was doing felt so good. He flicked his fingers against her slowly, and then with growing haste. She was rocking her hips against him in little, urgent movements, bunching the sheets in her hands, trying to find something to hold onto. "Take me, please," she whispered, almost at the point of tears.

His fingers stilled. "Are you sure?" he murmured, his voice low and full of dark temptation.

"Please," she moaned louder, panting hard. "Please, I need you."

The words were still on her lips, when she sat upright in bed—alone.

She blinked hazily, swaying, and realized that it had only been a dream. "A dream," she gasped, feeling the flush in her cheeks and the warmth still lingering in her body. It took her several moments to adjust to her wakened state, if one could call it that, for the image of her and Robert still played in her mind.

She swallowed hard, climbing out of the bed on shaky legs, and stumbled over to her dresser to find a dry nightgown. It was all she could do not to go down the hall, climb into bed with Robert, and re-create some of that dream.

But even as she glanced at her door, she realized the utter folly of what she was thinking—and finally she realized why. The older she became, the less likely it was that she would ever experience such things. As the years mounted and the suitors dwindled, the fact was that a happy marriage and a family of her own were the real dreams. And yet...

Perhaps she should speak to Robert about...a possible alliance. If Regina and Christopher did not find their way to each other again, nothing stood in the way of a different marriage. Perhaps their families could still be joined, even if it was not the way that they had intended. It was not too terribly far-fetched for the older siblings to marry; in fact, in hindsight, it may even have been a better idea than the original one to join Regina and Christopher.

Gwen shook her head at her own temerity. Such must be the dreams of old maids in the making.

"Stop your foolishness," she chided herself. She would end up taking care of her parents, and likely live in the home where she'd been born until the day she died.

She stared out the window into the star-pocked sky. As she watched, a cloud sailed slowly toward the moon and hit it, though neither seemed the worse for wear. Gwen sighed. Clearly, sleep had abandoned her for the night. Between musing on Miss Wilson and thinking about Robert, she would never rest. Maybe some warm milk would soothe her. She rang the bell pull at her bedside, and commenced to wait for Frances.

As she looked at the pile of journals, a sudden notion occurred to her. Perhaps she could sort out her worries and troubles by commending her own thoughts to a journal. For now she could start with pen and paper.

She rifled through the drawers of the dressing table, found paper, ink and quill and began to write.

*DEAR JOURNAL,*

*I am not quite sure what to make of this extended visit with Robert. He is becoming someone that I cannot say that I recognize—and that is a good thing, I think. He is helping me with Mrs. Thorne's journals; we have four more to review tomorrow after dinner and have pored through so many that I have lost count. He is so far from the man that I once thought he was. And the dreams that I'm having about him are most unbecoming; he's penetrating my thoughts, becoming someone that I think about daily, and apparently nightly.*

*I would almost say that I am beginning to feel something for Robert, though I thought I had made my mind up about him long ago. I would never have thought it possible; I am older than Regina and was beginning to feel that I would be unmarried forever, with her getting married first. Now, that appears as if it will not happen for my departed sister, and here I am with Robert nearly courting me. He follows me around and shows me the grounds, ensuring my comfort and safety at all times. I feel as if he is my shadow, my bodyguard, and my confidant.*

*Aside from Robert, I have heard things, noises, dim utterances coming from deep inside the hall. The door in my dressing room heads to the kitchen, I know—but why? When I listen close to it, I think I can hear muted sobbing and muffled words. I believe it is a woman's voice, but no one is in sight. I cannot discern where it is coming from; its source lies somewhere beyond the walls.*

. . .

AFTER A LONG MINUTE, she frowned and looked to the door. Usually Frances was much quicker than this. Could it be that she'd rung too late? Maybe the young girl was asleep and had not heard the bell. Slipping on her house shoes and wrapping her robe tightly around her, Gwen wandered out of her room. All was stillness in the hallway, and also in the house. It seemed she would have to get her own warm milk.

As she neared the top of the stairs, she saw Frances making her way up. "Oh, Frances," Gwen said. "I thought perhaps you were sound asleep."

Startled, the young maid dropped the rag she'd been carrying—and tripped.

"*Frances*," Gwen cried, grasping for her. Though Frances thrust out her hand, their fingers just missed.

As Gwen clutched the handrail, she watched in horror as Frances flailed her arms frantically. Her terrified gaze met Gwen's and then she fell backward, cartwheeling head over heel. She caromed down the steps, her body alternately doubling over or her limbs splaying out.

There seemed to be no stopping her as she gained speed, only to be halted abruptly by the stone floor far below. With a great thud, the limp body came to a rest.

"*Frances,*" Gwen shrieked, running down the stairs.

"What's going on?" she heard Robert shout from above.

But as Gwen reached the broken body of the young maid, the awful truth was only too clear: Frances was dead.

More shouts and thundering footsteps filled the air. Suddenly Robert was beside her, pulling her close. "My God, Gwen, what happened?"

Gwen covered her face with her hands as tears sprang into her eyes. "She tripped," she sobbed.

As she hid in the safe embrace of Robert's arms, he called for Parks to bring a sheet and told Agnes to stay back. When Jonathan arrived, he was sent for the doctor. Quiet finally descended and Robert softly asked, "Gwen, are you all right?"

She nodded tightly and swiped at her eyes, looking at Frances just as Parks finished covering her with a white linen.

Robert shielded her from the sight with his body. "Can you tell me what happened?" he asked. "How did she trip?"

"I...I'm not quite sure," Gwen said, looking back to the top of the stairs. "I had rung for her to order warm milk, and Frances had come. But she'd taken overly long and I'd assumed I would get it myself. I met her at the top of the stairs." Gwen gazed up at the steps. "There," she said pointing. "She dropped her rag because I think I startled her."

Parks hurried up the steps to fetch the rag.

Robert shook his head. "But surely being startled wouldn't have been enough to cause her to fall. She must have been up and down these steps hundreds of times."

Parks cleared his throat. "Sir, I believe there's something here you should look at."

As Robert joined him, Gwen followed.

"Careful of your step, Miss," Parks warned her.

Robert took her arm in a firm grip. "What have you found?" he asked his valet when they'd nearly reached the top.

Parks pointed at the step near the handrail. "Here, sir."

Robert carefully knelt and Gwen peered over his shoulder. The marble step was broken, its front edge almost neatly cleaved off. Though she was no stonemason, it seemed an improbable crack.

"The stone has fractured," he murmured. He ran his finger over the edge. "The break is crisp, and look here," he said pinching a few specks of what appeared to be white powder, "this is fresh stone dust."

As he stood, he motioned Parks back. "Back to the top," he said, and when the valet had retreated, Robert gingerly used one foot to try his weight on the remainder of the step. The front fractured off.

Gwen's hands went to her mouth. "Sabotage?" she gasped.

Robert nodded, his jaw tight and his eyes seeming to burn into the stone. "It would seem so."

* * *

DR. THACKERY HADN'T ARRIVED until well after midnight, but by that time Robert had managed to get Gwen to bed. To her credit she hadn't been hysterical, although she'd clearly been shaken, as had many of the servants. But he and Thackery agreed that if Gwen had gotten to sleep, there was no need for medicines or tonics.

As Jonathan and Parks stood by, the doctor examined Frances' body. Robert watched as the stout older man donned his spectacles and gently probed Frances' limbs and back, and then he examined her head.

"Mmm hmm," he muttered, and harrumphed through his mustache a few times, but, apparently satisfied, he stood and wiped his hands with a kerchief.

"Broken neck," he said. "She would have died immediately. Good thing, really. It was quick and relatively painless and better than begging as an invalid." He squinted and glanced up the stairs. "I presume she fell from up there?" Robert confirmed his guess and recounted all the details, including the broken marble. Thackery harrumphed again. "You think someone had reason to kill this girl? To kill the maid?"

"I sincerely doubt it," Robert answered.

"I think the malice might have been more... general in nature."

"Well," the doctor said, stowing his handkerchief in his leather bag and closing the top, "general or specific, I suggest you get that step fixed, and quickly." He eyed the body. "Have her people been notified?"

"I believe she had no family to speak of," Robert said quietly. "Isn't that right, Parks?"

"Yes, sir," he answered. "She was an orphan."

"She's for the potter's field then." As though the doctor had only just noticed the two men standing to the side, he waved a hand at them. "Put her in the back of my phaeton." Although Jonathan jumped to do the man's bidding, Parks looked at Robert.

"It's all right, Parks. Do as the doctor says."

"And the sooner, the better," Thackery said, pulling out his pocket watch and checking it.

Robert picked up the linen and watched as the two solemn men carefully lifted Frances and took her to the front entry doors, which Robert opened for them.

Thackery followed them through,

buttoning his overcoat and pulling the wide collar up high. "Damnable storm coming from the north," he grumbled.

After Parks and Jonathan had lain her on the floor of the rig, Robert covered her again with the linen. The doctor climbed up to the driver's seat and only glanced back to see that they were done, before snapping the reins and setting off.

Robert watched the phaeton disappear into the darkness before turning to his men. "Thank you both for your help. Please go get some sleep."

## CHAPTER 6

*R*obert spent the rest of the night in his library, pacing and creasing a small path in the rug. His breath came in shallow and sharp gasps and the scowl on his face was starting to feel permanent. Rage built upon rage in his chest until he stalked to the window and heaved it open. The frigid air filled his lungs and helped to clear his mind.

He had teased Gwen with her belief in ghosts, but now something had nearly happened to her—*twice*. Whether he liked it or not, and seemingly beyond his control, he was taking the threat of the supernatural much more seriously. He still didn't believe that ghosts existed, much less incorporeal beings that could tamper with marble steps, but something malevolent was at work.

He glanced behind him at the elegant dueling pistols mounted for display in one of the bookcases. Surely if someone intended harm, there were more direct methods than fractured marble steps.

After a long vigil at the window, Robert stalked back to his desk. Stacked upon it were several of the journals that Gwen had already finished. Perhaps she was on the right track, after all, in her quest to determine the fate of Miss Wilson and the Thornes. Was it possible that they had been the source of this evil?

When he'd put Gwen to bed, he had seen her own writing on the dressing table. He'd only just stopped himself from trying to glimpse a line or two when he thought better of it. Though he'd dearly like to know her private impressions, hopes, and plans, he knew it would be an intrusion.

Instead he would have to content himself with Mrs. Thorne's journals. He picked one up and began flipping through its pages. It was easy to see that she believed that she was purposely being driven insane. She claimed to have seen the courtesan hiding around corners, watching her. Mr. Thorne, of course, was said to have spent most of his nights with Miss Wilson, sneaking into her chambers and not leaving until the very early hours of the morning to return to his, which were separate from his wife's. She wrote that she had stalked the halls nightly, listening at the doors, not satisfied until she heard him go to bed.

"Poor disturbed woman," he muttered.

He recalled the letter from the courtesan that Gwen had found stuck in the middle of one of the journals. What was it that Miss Wilson had seen that made her think that she was going to be harmed? More importantly, who was attempting to harm her? He had his suspicions, of course, Mrs. Thorne chiefly among them.

"But was the poor woman's insanity of a lethal type?" he wondered.

But as much as he searched in her writings, some more lucid than others, there was no answer. Nor had he really expected one. They were journals, confidential musings at best, not indictments supported by fact. He closed the book and pushed it away.

If Mrs. Thorne had murdered Miss Wilson, or if Mr. Thorne had killed his wife to be with the courtesan, what kind of evidence could possibly show itself after all the years that had passed.

"Why am I even thinking about this?" Robert exclaimed, sitting back in his chair with a groan. "Gwen has gotten into my mind. I need to be thinking about this logically. Who or what could have possibly sabotaged the step that killed Frances?"

There was also still the matter of his chair, which had clearly been tampered with. Looking back, he couldn't discount the chandelier either, though they'd found no evidence of foul play. But taken together with the step and the chair, it only made sense that it had been the first instance of the unseen malevolent force.

But why? Always his mind returned to this central question. What possible reason could a person or even a ghost have for wanting to make Dredthorne seem haunted?

He wearily shook his head. It seemed

the night held no answers for him, only more questions. It was time to seek his own bed.

\* \* \*

THOUGH IT WAS WELL past the hour when Parks and the other servants should have been asleep, some of them were quite awake and gathered around the table in the back of the kitchen.

"I said it, didn't I?" Agnes said. "Frances looked like a young Miss Gwen, she surely did. And now the ghost went and claimed her by mistake. There's nothing else can be said about it."

Parks set down his tea. "I thought you didn't believe in ghosts, Agnes."

"Well, I didn't," she said quickly. "But now…"

This time Jonathan didn't argue, but nodded his head slowly. "You told Frances to look out. I never thought that you were telling the truth. I thought it was silliness and that nothing would ever come of it."

There was a general murmur of agreement around the table.

"The hall is cursed," Jonathan finally said. "It's true. And whatever protection the servants such as we had against it seems to have passed. The ghost is getting stronger and the blood lust of the damned is growing."

"Ridiculous," Parks said, trying to stem the rising tide of panic. Frances' death had come as quite the shock. "I saw those chair legs that fell out from under Mr. Sheraton, and those fractures in the marble stairs. Both were rigged. Someone living, someone flesh and blood is doing this." He rubbed his forehead with the back of his hand. "I'd help the master find out what's happening, but I don't know how."

"And so what if they were rigged?" Agnes said. "Is a killing person any less dangerous than a killing ghost?" Again there were murmurs of agreement from the rest. "And how could any murderer escape our eyes undetected? The master and mistress might not notice such things, but we would've seen any stranger coming and going."

"And which one of us worked here fifty years ago?" Jonathan demanded. "None, that's who. No, this is the work of a vengeful ghost or the devil himself, not a man." He visibly shivered and shook his head as if trying to throw off the trembling. "The appearance of tampering is just that. It's meant to deceive us."

"I have a cousin that knows something of the old ways," Agnes put in. "She knows the witching ways. Perhaps she could do something."

Jonathan shook his head. "The master would never allow it. He seems purposefully thick when it comes to anything he can't see or touch. But we know that a murderous phantom haunts these walls."

"Listen to yourselves," Parks said. "You sound like peasants who read chicken bones."

Agnes stood up, and took her tea cup with her. "Well maybe we are, Mr. Parks. But at least we'll be live ones."

Jonathan stood as well. "I see no choice, but that we must act accordingly."

## CHAPTER 7

The next morning, Gwen was reluctant to get out of bed. She stared up at the ceiling for a long time, trying to find some halfway reasonable excuse to stay there for the rest of the day. She was more confirmed than ever in her belief that the hall was haunted. Now it was only a matter of trying to convince Robert.

Even the weather seemed to want her to stay in bed. Outside a gale was raging, the force of the wind bending the trees like grass. It blew as if God himself had taken a breath in anger and released it into the world. Even at this hour, the sky was as black as coal. Her room was darker than she'd realized, so she rose and lit the candle.

Finally stirred to action for the sake of adding a little light to dispel the gloom, Gwen knew she must relent. She must join the day, such as it was. It was no time to hide away.

She struggled into her thickest dress, unused to dressing herself after having got used to Frances. Frances... She shuddered at the memory of the poor girl's death, and wrapped a shawl around her shoulders; to think Frances had been the victim of some malicious sabotage.

Gwen's gaze landed on the sheet of paper where she'd begun recording her own thoughts the previous night. She strode to the dressing table, and fetched a sheet of clean paper, before dipping her quill in the ink.

*DEAR JOURNAL,*

*Poor Frances, the maid, has died, and I might have been the cause. I'd rung for her so that I could order warm milk that might help me to sleep. But when she didn't come up, I started downstairs to make it myself. At the top of the stairs we almost ran into each other and I gave her quite the fright, so much so that she lost her footing and fell backwards to her death.*

*More than this, though, was the matter of the fractured marble. Though poor Frances had surely been frightened by my sudden appearance, the step upon which her foot had landed was ready to break. Robert is sure that the sabotage was intentional. I cannot say, for I am not an expert in such matters of masonry. But if it was, it was cunningly done.*

*It would seem then that the Ghost of Dredthorne Hall knows a thing or two about stonework. The malevolent phantom has finally managed to perpetrate its black will and kill someone. Had it not been for Frances coming up just as I was heading down, I might have been*

GWEN SET DOWN THE PEN, her hand shaking, and pulled the shawl tighter. Not only did she refuse to admit that she might have been the target of something malicious, but she refused to be daunted by it. Whatever was in store for her this day, she would have to go out and confront it.

In the hallway, except for the sounds of the storm, it was quiet. Carefully, and holding tightly to the handrail, she slowly made her way down the stairs, stepping over the damaged one, and taking each one after that one at a time.

Finally having successfully made her way down, she peered into the living room and found it was empty. Where was Robert? Each morning he liked to know what she had planned for herself that day; she liked knowing that perhaps her day meant more to him than it should. Not only was there no Robert, there was no breakfast. With a hand to her heart, she dashed to the kitchen—also empty.

All manner of thoughts flew through her mind. It seemed as though the entire hall was vacant. There were no sounds at all. Why would Robert leave her here in Dredthorne Hall by herself? As thunder boomed from above, tears sprang to her eyes.

But in the next moment, she went still. What if he hadn't abandoned her? What if he'd been killed or disappeared? What if all of them had?

As she stood unmoving, she felt a frigidly cold breeze stir a few tendrils of her hair. Where was that coming from? Again she ran and found herself in the entry hall, and then at the open front door.

Robert would never have been so careless, and neither would Parks, nor any of the other servants. A tremor ran down her spine as she peered through it. Driving rain and lashing wind made it almost impossible to see anything. But a sudden flash of lightning illuminated the entire front grounds and also the stable. There was a silhouetted figure standing in front of it.

"Robert?" she shouted.

If he'd made a reply, she wouldn't have been able to hear it. The wind was howling through the trees now and again thunder crashed. Standing in the doorway, she cupped her hands to her mouth and shouted for him again, but she could barely hear herself.

There was nothing for it. If she was going to find him—or whoever was at the stable—she would have to go there. She glanced back into the empty house and found that its dark stillness made up her mind. Nothing would keep her in the haunted hall by herself, not even a storm. She pulled her shawl as tightly around her as she could, then took a deep breath before she launched herself into the gale.

The wind whipped around her, sticks and leaves flying in every direction. Desperately she shielded her face with her hands, and only just managed to keep the torrent of rain from suffocating her. Placing one foot in front of the next, she trudged blindly forward in the direction of the stable. Puddles the size of small ponds had formed everywhere and in under a minute her shoes were sodden. But there was no thought of returning to the hall. She had to know if Robert was alive.

She squinted through the rain and found that she was nearly there. A shadowy form seemed to dance across the opening. Was that him?

"Robert!" she called, as loud as she could.

She began to run toward him but only managed two steps before she slipped and landed in the mud. With a great splash, she landed on all fours, her hands disappearing in the muck, and the rain drumming on her back. Suddenly there were a pair of boots in front of her face.

"Gwen!" Robert yelled. Despite her predicament, she almost wept with joy at the sound of his voice. She felt his strong arms around her waist as he lifted her to her feet. "Are you all right? What are you doing out here?"

"Looking for you!"

He hauled her into the stable and out of the blasted rain, where she took a moment to catch her breath and push her sodden hair out of her face.

"What are *you* doing out here?" she gasped. "The hall is empty."

"I know," he said. "I came to check that there was still a horse. The stable door had been left open, but we still have your horse and rig."

A sharp whinny punctuated his sentence, and she whirled to see her own mare, but the beast had a wild look in its eye.

"Gwen!" he cried out as he wrenched her to one side. In just the span of a breath, he'd interposed himself between her and the frightened horse. "Easy girl," he called out to the skittery animal, and held up his hands. "Easy now."

He seemed to be successfully herding her toward a stall when another bolt of lightning flashed outside. As the frightened mare leapt for the door, he flung himself at the opening and just managed to get it closed before she escaped. The animal reared up at the last second, kicking furiously. Though Robert nimbly jumped aside, as the mare came back down, one of her hooves caught his foot.

"Robert!" Gwen screamed.

Somehow her voice must have cut through the roar of the tempest, for the mare seemed to recognize it, turning toward her. Robert capitalized on the moment and, with a great shove, pushed the horse into the nearest stall, slamming the gate behind her.

"Gods," he muttered as he leaned back against the short wood door, and favored his injured foot.

"Are you hurt?" she said, running to him. "Is your foot broken?"

"It's my ankle," he said grimacing. "But I don't think it's broken."

She put her shoulder under his arm. "Do you think you can walk?"

"I must try," he said, and then took a faltering, heavy step. It seemed as though the ankle couldn't support much weight at all.

She pulled his arm around her neck. "You must lean on me, Robert. It's the only way we'll get back to the house."

"I fear you're right, dear Gwen," he said. "Nor do I think we can wait out this storm. While your mare will survive the chill, as rain-soaked as we are, we wouldn't make it half the day."

She nodded and tried to take more of his weight. "Then there's nothing for it."

As he limped and she staggered under his sizeable frame, they lurched to the stable door and managed to open it. Once through, the gale almost tore the door from their hands, but leaning into it with all their might, they shut and barred it.

"Good girl," he yelled above the wind and pelting rain. "We're halfway there now."

If only that were true, Gwen thought, saving her breath for the arduous walk. But step by heavy step, she steered them around the slippery mud and still growing puddles.

"Not quite the morning walk we usually enjoy," he said, breathing heavily.

As the entry to the hall finally came into sight, Gwen could hardly believe how utterly glad she was to see it. Her legs burned with the effort to support both their weights. Her arms ached and trembled from holding on to him so tightly. But finally, after what seemed to her like an eternity, they reached the house.

Slowly they lumbered up the steps, as Robert resorted to hopping on one leg for the last few. As they crossed the threshold, they collapsed together in a soggy heap, just inside the entry on the floor.

As the two of them stared at one another, open-mouthed and bedraggled, Gwen had to stifle a laugh. For no reason that she could fathom, she felt the impulse to giggle. Outside a storm and rampaging horse had nearly claimed their lives. Inside, they'd been deserted sometime in the night. With nothing else to do and no one to see them, Gwen suddenly felt light, as though a burden had been lifted.

She pushed herself up from the floor so she could at least sit. "You are a mess, Mr. Sheraton," she said, looking down at him and beginning to laugh.

At first he looked puzzled, but then the corner of his mouth crooked up in a half-grin. "Indeed." He sat up next to her and eyed her dress, particularly the thick coating of mud that clung to it. "And you, Miss Archer, are making a mess of the floor with that ruined dress of yours."

"I never liked it anyway," she said, prompting them both to erupt with laughter, just as another peal of thunder boomed, sending them into paroxysms.

As their mirth finally subsided, he took her hand. "Well I must confess that this dress is my favorite. The blue contrasts so nicely with your green eyes." Slowly he bent his head over her hand, and his lips lightly brushed her skin.

A flush of heat suffused her and the image from her dream flashed into her head.

"Robert," she said softly. As he looked

up into her face, she knew it must be crimson from the warmth radiating from it.

"Gwen," he said, leaning in so close that she could smell the fresh scent of rain in his hair. Startled, she realized that his eyes were not pure black. How had she never noticed the tiny flecks of hazel in them? As his face drew slowly closer, she could feel his soft breath on her lips. If he was going to kiss her it would have to be soon—before she melted.

"Sir!" came a voice from behind them. "Miss! I thought you'd gone."

\* \* \*

Relief washed over Parks as he ran down the entry hall. "I thought I was alone, sir." He bent to help up the master, who seemed to be having trouble standing. "Sir, you're hurt and…" He dried off his hands on his coat. "…soaking wet."

"It's a long story, Parks," Mr. Sheraton replied, "but I daresay we're quite glad to see you here." He reached toward Miss Archer. "Give me a hand."

Together they helped Miss Archer to stand. "Miss, you'll catch your death in these sodden clothes."

Though she'd been gazing into the master's eyes, she looked down at her spoiled dress and grimaced. "It is rather waterlogged."

"He's right, Gwen," Mr. Sheraton said, still holding her hand. "Do go up and change. I shan't be far behind."

Although she looked for a moment as though she might protest, she nodded her assent and made for the stairs with sloshing steps.

When the mistress was safely out of earshot, the master turned to him. "Where is everyone, Parks? I had to close the stable myself this morning and our horses are gone. Only Miss Archer's mare remains."

He wasn't quite sure how to put this. "The, uh, servants, sir. Well, they've…"

The master put his hands on his hips. "I can see the hall is empty, so out with it, man. What has happened?"

"They've quit, sir."

"*Quit?*" the master asked, his voice incredulous. "All of them? At once?"

"Yes, sir. I'm afraid so, sir." Parks waited for a response, and felt like he had to continue when none came. "It's just that... the investigations, sir. They've come up blank. No one can figure out how the chandelier and the chair became broken. And with Frances falling down the stairs and all..."

"I see," said the young master. Then to Parks' surprise, his countenance cleared. "I suppose it's to be expected really."

Emboldened by his reaction, Parks ventured the one thought that truly plagued him. "Perhaps Miss Gwen is right, sir. Perhaps Dredthorne is haunted, and something means to harm us."

"Do you really believe that?" Mr. Sheraton asked quietly, searching his face.

Parks lifted his hands. "Well, sir, it's just that I don't have a better explanation." There was the plain truth of it. He had never been a man prone to beliefs in the supernatural, in stories of ghosts and bogey men. But what other explanation did they have?

"In your time with the family, have you

ever heard of anything of the like before?"
Mr. Sheraton asked.

Parks nodded. "Not these exact
circumstances, no, sir. But strange things?
Yes, sir. About ten years ago, we had an
entire herd of horses stampede. They broke
down the fence, flew to the marshes and
got stuck and drowned. No one knew why.
Then a carriage wheel collapsed, also
without reason. The madam of the house
suffered fractured ribs. Agnes twisted her
knee climbing on a step stool to put away a
tureen. Pots of honey disappear, servants
hear voices. Strange things have always
happened at Dredthorne, but–"

"Well I'd hardly characterize a stampede
of frightened beasts and a carriage accident
in the same category."

Parks ducked his head. "You did ask,
sir."

"Of course, of course," Mr. Sheraton
said quickly. "Look, I think I'm going to
need a cane for this twisted ankle of mine.
Help me to the medical supply closet."

As Parks supported him under the
shoulder and they made their way down

the hallway, Mr. Sheraton asked, "Why did you stay, Parks?"

"I've served the Sheraton family all my life, sir," Parks told him. "I'd no sooner desert it than my own."

Not all household servants prized loyalty to the family—particularly not the younger generation—it was only too true. Their current situation spoke to the very fact. Although he didn't say it, Parks also had his pride. He could hardly think himself a man if Miss Archer stayed at Dredthorne while he ran away.

"Thank you, Parks," Mr. Sheraton replied. "I won't forget that." They reached the door to the supply closet and the master opened it. "Ah, here we are at last."

Inside were shelves of bandaging, metal basins, and glass bottles with labels that were faded but still legible. But in the corner, the master spied a cane.

"Yes," Mr. Sheraton declared, testing his weight on it. "This will do well." He clapped Parks on the shoulder. "Good man. My thanks again."

As Parks shut the door, he glanced at the master over his shoulder. "Beggin' your pardon, sir. There's no need to thank me just yet, on account of the fact that I can't cook without burning water."

As they walked side by side, back the way they came, Mr. Sheraton leaned heavily on the cane. "I see. So you're telling me that Miss Archer and I will have to fend for ourselves."

"Yes, sir. I'm afraid so, sir."

## CHAPTER 8

*A*s Gwen changed out of her sodden and filthy garments, she couldn't help but think that, if Parks hadn't interrupted them, Robert would have kissed her—and she would have let him. What a turnabout the years had brought. She thought suddenly of another rainy day, when she'd been only sixteen. A very different Robert Sheraton had made his feelings clear.

Gwen sat on the back patio of the Sheraton estate with her sister, Regina, as their parents discussed something of grave importance inside. Regina was laughing as she chattered on and on with Christopher, who had brought her a small bouquet of daisies. Gwen sat nearby with a large tome that she couldn't for the life of her focus on—especially when Robert joined them.

She had never met someone quite like Robert Sheraton. He was slightly older than her, and very attractive with his jet black hair and mysterious dark eyes. But more than that, he exuded an air of quiet certainty, as if he already knew his path in life. Perhaps it was to be expected as he was the older of the two brothers. In some sense, his role was decided.

He sat on a bench at the edge of the patio with his own book, while Regina giggled with Christopher. As Gwen idly flipped the pages of her volume, she watched Robert out of the corner of her eye. He seemed genuinely fascinated with what he was reading until he apparently felt her eyes on him.

"May I help you, Miss Archer?" he said, his reproachful tone drawing everyone's attention.

The heat in Gwen's cheeks told her that she must be blushing, but she wasn't going to simply let his remark go unanswered.

"I was just wondering what...you are

reading," she said, nearly cringing at her own words.

"Were you indeed," he retorted. He showed her the volume of Sir Walter Scott's poems from her father's library. "Here," he said, "let me quote a particularly apt section to you." Glancing down at the page, he put his finger on a certain line. "Oh! What a tangled web we weave, When first we practice to deceive!"

When Regina tittered, Gwen glared at her, before slamming her book shut, and marching indoors.

Even now, the embarrassment of that long ago moment colored Gwen's cheeks. He'd seemed to her unreservedly haughty and quite mean. In the intervening years, she'd convinced herself of it.

But now—she glanced at the ruined dress on the floor—she had to wonder.

THOUGH IT WAS good to get into a set of dry clothes, Robert didn't relish confronting the grim truth with Gwen. She'd been marvelous out in the storm, if a bit reckless, and he'd come very close to kissing her. If he wasn't mistaken, she'd even been amenable to it. But the perfect moment had been lost and the heavy responsibilities of his family, and now the entire hall, had returned and settled him back to the earth.

When he checked her chambers and found them empty, he used his cane to proceed down to the secret library that had seemingly become a second home to her. But to his surprise, she wasn't there. Even more disconcerting was the smell of food coming from the kitchen. Though he'd half-expected to find Parks there, despite what the man had said, he could scarce believe he saw Gwen at the stove. Over her white dress, she wore the cook's apron, and stood in front of two large iron skillets.

"Gwen," he exclaimed. "You cook?"

"I wouldn't say that," she said over her shoulder. "As you can see."

In one skillet she was frying bacon and in the other eggs, though none of the yolks remained whole, and the bacon had burnt on one side.

"Let me help," he said, taking down a

large fork hanging from a hook. "I'll flip the bacon."

"I'm afraid I've built the fire unevenly and the pan is too hot in the middle," she pointed out.

As she stepped aside to attend to the eggs, he used the fork to turn the thick cuts of back bacon, only to find himself instantly splattered with grease.

"Perhaps we should switch," she suggested. "I have the apron." As they did, he felt the light brush of her dress across his legs. "Where is Parks?" she asked.

"I've asked him to chip away the fractured portions of that stair step," he said, and then paused. "Did he tell you that the rest of the servants have deserted?"

She began to plate the eggs on an oval silver platter. "No, but it didn't take much guessing on my part to come to that conclusion." She put a few eggs and slices of the meat on a separate plate. "We'll save some for him."

"Well," Robert said, as they took their food to the makeshift table in the living room, "it's very good of you to do this." He rested the cane against an empty chair and held her seat for her.

She smiled up at him as she sat. "I was hungry."

For several minutes they devoured their simple meal in silence. In fact, Robert couldn't remember the last time he'd had eggs or bacon that he'd enjoyed so much. He poured two cups of tea from the china pot that was already on the table.

"Look, Gwen," he finally said. "I can't leave Dredthorne in case Christopher should arrive. There's no point in me returning to London to conduct a search from there. I must stay until this matter is closed." He looked directly into her light green eyes, distracted for a moment before he could continue. "But you should return to Renwick. Without servants, there'll only be more hardships."

When she'd finished sipping her tea, she set it down with purpose. "I'm not leaving," she said simply, but firmly. "Regina is still missing as well. As you can see," she indicated their empty plates with her eyes, "I can manage well enough. Because my father is not able to keep as many servants as Dredthorne has—or had—I have learned a few of the domestic skills of necessity."

He looked at her with a renewed sense of wonder. "Is there anything that you cannot do? Any situation you cannot remedy?"

She blushed a little, flushing her cheeks with a most attractive shade of pink. "If I could bring our siblings to us, I would," she said. "But since I can't, we must make our wait as pleasant as may be. I'll look into the house records and make a plan for Parks to go down into the village. Though rumors of the doings here at the hall may preclude our finding servants there, we might send word to London."

Something in the tone of her voice, and her easy determination, spoke volumes of what her home life must have been. She was in her element, he decided, and clearly relished it.

Despite his aching ankle and the storm just now waning outside, he found himself relaxing for the first time in days. It was as though the extra responsibilities thrust upon them buoyed her up.

It also occurred to him that the new

chores left no time to muse on malevolent spirits. But at any rate, she was right. As long as they continued to wait for his brother and her sister, or at least receive word from them, they should make their stay as pleasant as was possible.

## CHAPTER 9

*T*hough it had taken hours of wading through Dredthorne Hall's payroll registers, Gwen had compiled a list of the servants that it typically employed. First came the steward to look after Robert and manage all the other servants. Clearly this was a role that Parks could fulfill. Under him, the butler was the head of the male servants, while the housekeeper supervised the women. Below them came valets and lady's maids. Gwen's heart had to clench at the thought of Frances' fate. But more important than any of those positions, they needed a cook. That was to be Parks' first priority, something on which they'd all agreed. The footmen as well as the chamber, kitchen, and scullery maids could all wait, as could the outdoor staff.

With a letter posted to her parents, another from Robert to his mother, and a list of provisions they'd need, Parks had left in her rig when the weather had cleared. Until he returned, she had decided to create a proper journal for herself.

In the secret library, she'd found an empty daybook among the used ones. Though it'd taken a bit of time to transfer her existing entries on the sheets of paper into them, she looked down on the slender leather bound book with satisfaction. Only now, seeing it here with the others, did it occur to her that she might be leaving her mark on the history of the hall. It inspired her to take pen in hand.

*Dear Journal,*

*All of the servants, save Parks, have deserted us. Add to that the fact that Robert suffered a twisted ankle while trying to calm my horse during the morning's storm. Yet for reasons that I cannot fathom, I do believe we are equal to the task of managing the hall.*

*Robert has been nothing but supportive, encouraging me to do as I like. I feel almost as if I were the actual mistress of this dark place. For the first time it seems as though I have a clear path forward.*

*But of all the changes that have happened here today, one in particular comes to my mind again and again. As we sat in the entry way of the hall, soaked with freezing rain, I believe Robert meant to kiss me. It was the most thrilling moment of my life. Even now, I can feel the warmth of his breath on my mouth.*

SHE SET down her pen slowly and touched her lips with trembling fingers. What would it be like to kiss him? Would he be demanding and willful, subduing any doubts that might linger with her? Or would he be tender and full of gentle entreaties that she couldn't resist? When she realized that she was stroking her own lips, she quickly clasped her hands together.

"Stop your nonsense," she muttered to herself. She stood and went to the window in the adjoining dining room.

Though the storm had abated, the sky was still completely gray. Windblown leaves covered the ground, and the stark boughs and branches of winter reached for the sky. Gwen folded her arms around herself, suddenly chilled.

"Wherever you are, Regina," she said quietly, "I hope you are safe."

Her sister had always enjoyed this type of wild weather, though Gwen could never understand why. But as she remembered those days, when Regina had run through the rain, a thought occurred to her that made her smile. She imagined her sister on some fine adventure. Perhaps she was seeking her fortune, drifting wherever the winds would take her, laughing and living as she chose. Or perhaps she'd joined a traveling band of actors. It wasn't an exploit that was too far out of the question, with her sister's flair for the dramatic. Regina had always found it easy to make friends with everyone she met.

Regina had been vivacious and free-spirited. She'd been–

Gwen stopped herself. She was thinking of her sister in the past tense.

Though she hadn't wanted to admit it, this was the worry that had burrowed deep into her soul: What if Regina was dead?

Tears burned in her eyes as she remembered the outlandish girl who snuck out during the night to go dancing with her friends; the girl who'd run barefoot; the girl so full of life that she simply couldn't be dead.

She'd been envious of her sister, something she had to admit now. When her father had announced Regina's betrothal to Christopher, it'd broken her heart. She'd always dreamt that they two would get married in the same ceremony, but how could Gwen marry Robert when her sister married his brother?

Gwen shook her head. It did no good to tread over old ground, no good at all. She cast a look back into the secret library. The journals always took her mind off her troubles. She hurried back to them and picked up one in which she'd placed a book mark. It was Mrs. Thorne's.

*DEAR JOURNAL* –

*During this last month I've begun to see shadows in the halls. I know that it's Miss Wilson, come to steal Mr. Thorne from me. I see her hair whipping around corners, hiding her from my staring eyes. She haunts the hall with every step she takes. She's taking him away from me, and I am coming to realize that I must do something about this, lest I lose him forever.*

*He's going away on a trip for his businesses soon, to London. Is he taking her with him? Is he taking me with him? I can feel the fear creeping up my skin like so many spiders. I have heard nothing but whispers from the servants that scuttle along the hallways with the mice, so quiet, waiting for me. There is one passage in particular that brings me to the kitchen that I like to listen at, to find out such things.*

*I am hunting like the spiders that I see in the hallways. I hunt for knowledge, for wisdom. I will find out what is happening in my home.*

BARELY FEELING HIS ANKLE, Robert paced restlessly in his library at the thought of his vanished brother. But it wasn't his brother's fate that worried him now, but his own.

How dare Christopher leave him here alone with Gwen?

When he'd stood with her in the kitchen and her dress had brushed his legs, it'd taken every ounce of self-control within him not to grasp her about the waist. Even though she'd worn the cook's apron, she'd never looked lovelier. When they'd sat at breakfast, it'd been as if they'd done so as a married couple, so comfortable in each other's company.

Whatever came their way, they seemed up to the task. Where he lacked, she excelled. Where she was inexperienced, he had the practical knowledge.

Didn't his brother know that every moment he spent with the woman was utter torture? He'd come here to accept Gwen's message on behalf of Christopher, and nothing more. Yet here he was, trying to charm the woman of his dreams, determined that he would win her over.

Something deep within his soul said the one thing he dare not speak out loud: *Gwen must be his wife.*

As he'd watched his brother's infatuation for Regina grow, he'd never had the courage to speak of his own. Instead, he had been a royal ass to Gwen, barely tolerating her presence because he was too afraid to say what was in his heart. It had taken Christopher's engagement to Regina to make him realize what a mistake he'd made.

But he would set that to rights, before their stay at Dredthorne Hall was over, he'd set that to rights.

## CHAPTER 10

*G*wen sat in her bedchamber, about to open one of the last remaining journals, when she heard Robert's voice out in the hall.

"A message?" he was saying. "From whom?"

She emerged to see Parks at the top of the stairs, his coat dripping with rain. The poor man was shivering. Bless him for going to Renwick in such weather.

"From your family, I was told, sir," Parks said, handing over the letter.

Robert took it and said, "Thank you, Parks. That will be all. Go warm yourself by the fire."

"Thank you, sir," he said with a small bow. He nodded quickly to Gwen, "Miss."

Scowling, Robert opened the letter. He read it slowly, once, and then twice. Looking up at her he said nothing but she saw the blood drain out of his face.

"*Robert*," she said, going to him and taking his hand. "What is it?"

He held out the message to her, and she read it quickly, her hand flying to her chest. "Oh, Robert," she whispered, her voice catching. "I'm so sorry."

His mother had written to inform him that his father had died, and that her sister, Robert's aunt, had joined her.

Robert's eyes glistened with unshed tears. "I knew Christopher's disappearance would be too much for him. I shouldn't have told him."

She shook her head, reaching up to cup his cheek with her palm. "It isn't your fault," she whispered. "You did what you had to do, what any responsible son would have done. You had to prepare him for even more tragic news, should it come. Keeping the truth from him would have served no purpose. He was already gravely ill."

"Yes," he whispered and nodded, though

he didn't sound convinced. "I'm sure you're right."

"I am," she said, "because I always am." She smiled up at him. "So I'm afraid there's nothing for it but to believe me."

"Ah, my dearest Gwen," he said, putting his hand to her cheek. "How I wish it were that simple."

As she gazed into his shimmering eyes, the sadness there broke her heart. Tears sprang into her own eyes as she turned her face to his palm and placed her lips there.

He took in a sharp breath and then didn't move. She felt his gaze as surely as if it had been a heated brand. When she finally dared to look up at him, he took her by the shoulders and slowly drew her to him. In moments only inches separated their lips, as though an unstoppable force attracted them.

Warmth suffused her, as it had just after the storm, heated by his touch and his nearness. He was so close that his breath brushed across her lips and her head filled with his musky sweet scent. If he were to stop now, she thought she might go mad, but then his lips pressed into hers. She wavered a moment, before she surrendered to him, wrapping her arms around him to steady herself.

As though she'd unlocked something in him, he ravished her with his mouth, his tongue flicking against her lips. She opened to him, melting against his body as he swept his tongue against hers. His strong arms wrapped around her waist and she moaned softly, as his body pressed into hers.

He shuddered and then did the unthinkable, pulling away slowly. Gwen looked up at him through heavy lids, feeling as dazed as he looked. Her breath came in ragged snatches, and she saw his nostrils flare.

He rested his forehead against hers. "You must be sure, Gwen," he whispered hoarsely. "For I am sure that I will not be able to stop."

She could feel him pressing against her skirts, his flesh so hard that it took her breath away. "I am sure," she gasped. "I have dreamt of this moment."

In one smooth motion he reached down and swept her off her feet before she knew what was happening. In the next moment they were in her bedchamber, and he kicked the door closed behind him. As he lay her on the bed, his mouth found hers again, hungry and insistent, kissing her breathless. Her fingers fumbled with his shirt, trying to untuck it from his trousers, until his lips released hers.

Tremors ran down her spine as he stood and began to strip, throwing his coat to the floor, and tearing his shirt off over his head. Mesmerized, she watched him, as the hard planes of his gorgeous chest were revealed. Suddenly he was back on the bed with her, reaching behind her to unbutton her dress. Her fingers roamed over the smooth flesh of his chest and the hard ridges of his stomach. She could feel his hands shaking, but when he finally undid the last button, she forced herself to push him away. If he was going to undress her it would take forever. She stood, and in short order she removed her dress, petticoat and stays, until only the thin linen chemise and stockings remained.

"I would see you, Gwen," he growled, stepping to her and lifting the chemise up and over her head. Cool air swept down her body, tightening her bare nipples. "You're so beautiful," he murmured, as he went to his knees and laved her belly with kisses.

Heat flooded between her thighs, as she carded her fingers through his thick hair. She kneaded the bunched muscles of his shoulders and his hands softly squeezed her breasts. A wild tremor suffused her core as the aching need between her legs pulsed so fiercely that she nearly lost her balance.

"Robert," she gasped. "I need you." When his fevered eyes gazed up at her, she could see that he felt the same. "Show me yourself."

He needed no other urging. As he stood and stripped off his boots and trousers, his thick length sprang free. She stared at the heavily veined flesh with its satiny, engorged head, and couldn't imagine how it would feel. Slowly he moved her back toward the bed, and then lowered them both to it, as he settled down between her thighs. But instead of bringing that rod of flesh to the wetness between her legs, his clever fingers found her opening and one slipped inside.

With a sudden gasp, Gwen felt her face burn and tried to bury it in his chest. She'd never felt anything so thrilling and yet no other man had ever seen her naked, let alone touched her there.

"No shame, Gwen," he whispered, and lifted her chin. "Not here. Not with me."

His fingers were gentle against her opening, spreading her slick folds. But when they circled the little nub of her sex, her hips bucked in response.

"Robert," she cried out, arching into his palm. She hadn't known it could be like this, yearning for something she couldn't name. Her nails dug into the bed and her hips pushed against his hand. *"Please, Robert."*

But when it was clear that he had no intention of stopping the onslaught of pleasure, her fingers found his hot shaft and he moaned. Robert pulsed in her hand, and for a moment her entire world became Robert's panting breaths and her pitiable moans. As a thick warmth spread low in her belly, she stroked his length with her fist.

Finally he took his fingers from her and replaced her fist with his own, and he guided himself to her opening. The dome of his erection pressed against her, spreading her with a delicious stretch.

"Are you sure?" he breathed.

"Yes, Robert, yes," she answered, her voice trembling as her body shook with need. "Take me now."

Hesitating for the briefest moment, he slowly pushed inside her. Her legs instinctively wound around his hips and he pressed even further into her. It was glorious, and so much more than she could have dreamt. It was as though their bodies had been meant for each other. The slow glide of him into her core, only made her want him all the more. She clenched around him, urging him further. He hissed sharply in response, burying himself to his root.

"Gods," he rasped. "You feel so good."

All she could do was whimper in response and clutch his shoulders. As he withdrew and then entered her again, her hips flexed eagerly, her body convulsing softly around him as they began to move together.

"Oh, yes," she breathed, and her head fell back limp against the pillow. She understood now why lovers would do anything for this time together. Ecstasy and carnal hunger like she'd never known unfolded inside her. He stoked a rhythmic fire in her hips, and she fueled his faster penetrations.

She was screaming now, crying as she met him thrust for thrust. Suddenly, as pleasure blossomed in her belly and spread up through her breasts, she clenched around him. He swore, crying out with her as she relentlessly milked him, until finally he grunted and released his hot seed deep inside of her.

Though tremors of passion still rocked them, they finally slowed until there was only the sound of their ragged breaths. Though her body still thrummed from the fierce climax, he slowly rolled to his side and gently brought her with him.

"Heavens," she swore in disbelief, eyes

half-closed. Nothing had ever, or could ever, feel so good.

He gazed down at her as his fingertips traced her jaw. "I've loved you from the moment I met you," he said quietly. "I'm only sorry that I didn't tell you sooner."

"You what?" she asked, surprised. "But you—"

"Treated you unkindly, my dear Gwen. Because I was too afraid to say what was in my heart, I pushed you away."

She stared at him now. "And what is in your heart?"

"Only and ever this," he said, gazing into her eyes. "Will you marry me, Gwen?"

A tremor shot down her spine and she blinked. She had truly never thought to hear those words. Yet now that she had, she could hardly believe them—and the doubt that crept into her mind. Perhaps he was being carried away by the moment. Or perhaps it was the shock of his father's death. Perhaps he even sought to act the gentleman and keep her from shame.

"I…want to make sure that's what we both want," she said, "before I give you an answer."

He said nothing, but gathered her up in his arms, as she nestled against him. They lay like that together until a deep sleep finally claimed them both.

* * *

ROBERT HAD TAKEN her again in the afternoon, until she lay completely limp in his arms. They'd fallen asleep like that, with him still inside of her, as he planned to do from now to the end of their days.

At some point during the night, she had turned to her side. Now, with his head propped up on his hand, he watched her sleep as the sun of a new day rose. Her fingertips twitched as she dreamed, and he slid his hand into hers, holding it gently.

"I love you," he whispered softly, knowing that she could not hear him.

He looked out the window to the growing brightness. It was not just a new day, it was a new juncture in his life, for he had finally declared himself for the woman he loved and had asked for her hand. No matter what came now, he felt his life had finally taken its true course. Though Gwen had demurred from giving him an answer, he would not pressure her. For the only thing that could make him happier than he was at this very moment, was to have her as desirous of a marriage as he was.

As light slowly filled the room, she stirred and opened her beautiful eyes. Her gaze darted one way and then another as if she didn't remember where she was, and then she blushed.

"Good morning," he whispered softly, smiling down at her.

She lowered her gaze. "Good morning," she said shyly.

With the tips of his fingers he tilted her chin up. "No shyness, no shame, Gwen," he said, echoing his words from the previous day. "Not with me. Not ever."

As she half rose, he thought that she meant to leave him, but instead she tugged the blankets up over their shoulders, and curled into his body. With relief, he wrapped her up in his embrace.

"No shame," she whispered. "It's just that I think I might love you."

A grin burst across his face and his chest swelled. Though he knew he had to be smiling like a giddy school boy, he didn't care. She had admitted what he'd known all along: that they were meant for each other.

She hid her flushing face against his chest, and Robert grinned again. Her shyness was adorable, and he could feel her smiling against him. As he looked down at her, stroking her hair, he noticed a small mark on her neck—from him. It stirred him, and he shifted against her. But as he nuzzled behind her ear, her stomach suddenly gurgled loudly in the silence of the room.

She clutched at it as though she could hide the fact. But then his did the same, as though she'd reminded him of how little they'd eaten.

Yesterday had been a whirlwind. First had come the tragic news that had devastated him, but then had come his beautiful Gwen and their glorious love-making. Only one matter still separated them.

"I know you have yet to give me your answer," he said gravely. "But I'm afraid we have a more pressing question."

She pulled back to look up at him. "Robert, what is it?"

"Who is going to cook the bacon?" he said, and then grinned.

"*Oh, you,*" she exclaimed and thumped his chest, as he laughed and pulled her atop him.

## CHAPTER 11

*A*s Gwen fried the spattering bacon, Robert came up behind her with the basket of eggs, and wrapped an arm around her waist.

"I like to think of this as practice for when we can have a small house of our own," he said. "It'd be a charming country cottage where we wouldn't need any servants. It would be just the two of us, together."

Gwen could think of nothing more pleasant in all the world, but she kept silent. Even now she could still not quite believe that they'd made love, and that he'd actually proposed.

She had to remind herself that he might not be quite in charge of his emotions. He'd only just had a great shock with the death of his father. Were she to accept him and they married, would he quickly regret his hasty decision? It was all a muddle in her mind. Perhaps her reservations were shared by all prospective brides. If only she could consult with Regina. She would surely know.

Gwen's brow furrowed as the thought of her vanished sister sent a twinge of guilt into her chest. Here she was, enjoying domestic bliss, while her sister was still missing.

When Robert nuzzled the side of her neck, she patted his arm. "Before we plan a household, perhaps we should see to breakfast. The pan for the eggs is just here."

As he moved to her side, she stole a glance at him. How happy and peaceful he looked as he went about cracking each egg into the pan.

She glanced down at his feet. "You no longer need your cane," she observed.

"No," he agreed. "It would seem that... um...not being on my feet most of yesterday has seen to its quick mending."

She smiled a little as she turned back to

the stove. "Did you encounter Parks on your way to the chicken coop?"

Robert nodded. "Indeed I did. It was he who collected this morning's new eggs." He smiled at her. "He was good enough not to inquire as to our whereabouts yesterday."

"No new servants yet I suppose," she said, flipping the bacon.

"I'm afraid not," he confirmed, his smile fading. "It would seem Dredthorne Hall's reputation has preceded it."

When he finished with the eggs, he also managed to find bread and make some toast. Once again they breakfasted at the makeshift dining table, drinking the weak tea that Robert had made. The toast was only slightly burned so they ate their fill as they chatted about the weather and wondered how the kitchen gardens were faring without a gardener. It was as though they were determined to return to some type of normalcy. But even as they talked about inconsequential things, his idea of having a little house together was growing more interesting by the moment.

"What are you going to do today?" Robert asked, before making a face into his cup. "I really do need to learn how to make a decent cup of tea. This is horrible."

"You didn't steep it long enough," she said. "And the water was not hot enough. I think I'm going to set the journals into order by date. It's clear that Mrs. Thorne's illness had much to do with whatever happened afterwards. What I'd like to find out is whether she died, when Miss Wilson disappeared, and what Mr. Thorne had to do with all of this." He nodded. "And you?"

Now his expression turned grim, a bleak reminder of yesterday's news. "I must reply to my mother." He reached across the table and took her hand in his. "I know that we would both like to stay here for the sake of our wayward siblings, but my father's....funeral will not be delayed long. I will not leave you alone here, Gwen."

"Nor would I stay," she declared. "No, I shall return to Renwick to give my parents the awful news in person that I must abandon the search for Regina, if indeed that is what happens." Robert's face fell but she gripped his hand more tightly. "Of course we shall come to you in London, to meet your mother and pay our respects at your father's service."

"Thank you, dearest Gwen," he said, squeezing her hand.

Together they took the dishes to the scullery kitchen's sink, where he paused to look at her. Though his eyes roamed over her face and lingered on her mouth, he simply took her face in his hands and gently kissed her forehead.

"I must write that letter," he said, holding her at arm's length for a second before letting her go. "Then I will send it with Parks and see what needs to be done in the stable."

As she watched him leave, she nearly called him back. Though she didn't feel she could give him an answer, parting from him simply made her heart ache. But as they'd said, there were things to do, so she took off her apron, hung it on the peg where she'd found it, and went to the secret library.

Before she began arranging the leather-bound books in order, however, she picked up one of the later ones that still lay open and read it again.

. . .

*DEAR JOURNAL –*

*I have found Mr. Thorne! He was indeed in London. I needn't have worried. But that slattern Miss Wilson has commenced in haunting my lonely halls. I find strands of her hair in my hairbrush, I can smell her scent on my husband. When he and I make love, I know that he is thinking of her. He is so very distracted and he claims that it is business matters, but I know better.*

*There has to be a way to get him back. The shadows are creeping closer to me, watching every movement I make. I don't know how she's sending the shadows to me, but I know that it is her. There are no other answers. They watch me as I undress, as I spend time with Mr. Thorne, and part of me begins to wonder if the shadows are not her, but him. Perhaps it is he that wants me so troubled and worried.*

*As I think on it, it seems even more possible that my husband would want to trick me into this insanity, make me question and worry about my mind. Perhaps he is punishing me for not giving him his child.*

. . .

IT WAS FRIGHTFULLY clear to Gwen that the poor woman was in the grips of something, be it madness or illness. From this vantage point in time, she couldn't tell which. But something was deeply troubling Mrs. Thorne, even if it was just an illness that caused her to see things that were not there.

Gwen smoothed a finger over the text. Could illness and madness really be confused for one another, she wondered, and closed the book. As she looked across the table surveying the collection of journals, there were only a few facts that were undisputed: a courtesan had joined the Thornes at Dredthorne; Mrs. Thorne had died; Miss Wilson had gone missing. Everything else was speculation.

Even so, Gwen felt in her heart that the answers were somewhere on the table before her. But before she undertook her task, she decided to commit some thoughts to her own journal.

As she sat down to write, she paused for a moment, contemplating what needed to be written.

·  ·  ·

*Dear Journal,*

*Yesterday, Robert and I made love for the first time, and then again. I find myself more than smitten with him. Truthfully, I know what my answer will be to his proposal, but I cannot find it in myself to say it just yet. I am frightened to commit to this course without knowing for sure that he is committed for the right reasons.*

*I know that Robert wouldn't hurt me on purpose, but could he hurt me accidentally?*

*What does his mother think? Does she even know that Robert had feelings for me when he left? I cannot imagine that she wouldn't know. He told me that he had had feelings for me from the start, even before our parents decided that Regina and Christopher should become betrothed.*

*I wonder what would have happened if they had arranged for Robert and I instead. We seem quite suited for each other; even in the disaster of having all of the servants desert us, we are managing quite well in such a large place. If I try, I might even remember how to sew!*

*But I also can't help but think that, though we are not married, our union will mean that the curse descends on me.*

. . .

JUST THEN THE barely audible sound of a moan drifted to her. Gwen went still, straining to hear it. It'd been days since she'd heard the dim sobs and moans, and without realizing it, she'd almost convinced herself that they hadn't been real. But there it was again. She was sure of it. Though she waited an interminable period and even held her breath, the sound didn't come again.

"Could it have been the wind?" she whispered, looking out of the secret library to the dining room windows. But the sky was clear and the trees were still.

She put a shaky pen to her journal.

*I HAVE HEARD the noise again. Does it mean that I'm already going mad, and just do not know it yet?*

\* \* \*

AFTER PARKS HAD LEFT to post his letter, Robert took the opportunity to attend to the stable without the mare in her stall. As he expected, the enclosure badly needed to be mucked out. Robert donned Jonathan's high boots, though they were a bit tight, and fetched the shovel and fork that had been hanging with the other tools, putting them in the wheelbarrow that he rolled to the stall.

Despite the odious smell, Robert took a strange comfort in the task. Because Parks had been watering and feeding Gwen's mare, Robert hadn't been to the stable since that day in the storm. It felt good to be outdoors, and it occurred to him that perhaps Gwen and he should take a turn around the gardens later.

For now though he simply shoveled the muck into the wheelbarrow, and when it was full he took it outside and dumped it in the manure pile. When the shoveling was complete, he looked around for fresh bedding, but there was none in the stable. Though he'd barely taken notice of them before, Robert remembered the haystacks that were stored in the barn next door. It turned out the wheelbarrow was a handy tool.

What had begun as a simple wish to make sure that the horse's hooves were dry was turning into quite the day. Using the pitchfork, he not only loaded the wheelbarrow with hay, but used the same implement to spread it in the stall. As he replaced those tools in their respective places, his gaze fell on the wide broom. A glance at the various paths he'd used during his mucking and fetching hay showed him that he'd added to the mess left by the storm.

As he swept away the debris, he recalled his conversation with Gwen in the kitchen. Is this what his days would become if they found some pleasant country house to make their own? If going home to Gwen every evening meant he'd muck stalls every day, it'd be a price he would gladly pay.

He imagined their days together, in that nonexistent country house. There would be bacon and eggs every morning, and her in his bed every night. How quickly she had responded to him, giving herself completely. Every inch of her had proved as luscious as he'd—many times—imagined.

But the intense joy of their love-making had truly taken him by surprise. He would fill her with it, with him, until she screamed his name again. He could still hear it on her lips, and his cock swelled in response.

The sound of horse hooves clattering on the brick drive, stopped his reverie. When Robert went outside, he saw that Parks had returned.

"Sir, is that you there in those boots?" his valet called to him.

Robert waved. "Yes, Parks. I got it in my head to get some physical activity. It does no good to brood indoors."

Robert watched Parks maneuver the rig inside, and helped him to unhitch the mare. Then he took her bridle and led the sweaty horse into the newly cleaned stall.

Although he intended to wipe her down and brush her, Parks handed him a bundle of envelopes and papers.

"What's this?" he asked.

"Your father's steward has sent these to you, sir," his valet replied. "I was told to bring them to you immediately."

Of course. Now that his father was

dead, Robert was the head of the household.

"I'll attend to the mare and the rig, sir," Parks said.

With a sigh, he set the bundle of papers aside while he changed his boots, and then took them into the house where he found Gwen in the secret library standing next to the table of journals. It looked as though she'd arranged them into two rows.

"Gwen, you're still here?"

She brushed a stray tendril of hair from her forehead. "Yes," she sighed, sounding exasperated. Then she saw the bundle in his hands. "What do you have there?"

"Papers from my father's steward," he said setting them down. "No doubt there are bills for the household in London to be paid, correspondence to be read, and investments to monitor." He glanced down at the table. "What have you found?"

Crossing her arms in front of her, she frowned. "I think that Mr. and Mrs. Thorne were having marital problems." She glanced at one of the rows. "Mr. Thorne was always away for business, and having the courtesan at the hall was too much for

Mrs. Thorne. She'd begun to feel like Mr. Thorne was in love with Miss Wilson. Shortly after the entry where she wrote about her suspicions, she took sick."

"What happened?"

She pointed to the second row. "Mr. Thorne started a journal at the time she fell ill. But the journals tell very different stories to those of his wife. He writes that he had begun to stay at the hall *more* to care for her, and that he had sent Miss Wilson to town with the steward to collect some medications for her when the courtesan went missing." She pointed to the first row. "While Mrs. Thorne said that she never saw her husband again, and that he ran away with Miss Wilson. In fact, she believed Miss Wilson and her husband were trying to kill her. At about the same time, Mr. Thorne's journal says that his wife succumbed to madness and illness." She threw up her hands. "Then they both end, without any way to resolve them."

Robert frowned. "So who do we believe?" he asked. "It's clear that either way, Beatrice Thorne passed on. But what took her? Mr. Thorne and his courtesan, or an illness? And what happened to the courtesan after everything else?"

"I don't know," she replied. "I'm going to see if there are any records of Mrs. Thorne's passing in the house. Perhaps that's one question we can sort out."

"All right," he said. "What can I do?"

"You can contact the doctor," she said, surprising him. "I was going to send a letter, but I don't know his name. Maybe he had a mentor, or perhaps one of his predecessors cared for Mrs. Thorne and there are medical records somewhere."

"His name is Dr. Thackery and I think that's a wonderful idea. I'll write to him immediately." When she didn't respond, he asked, "Is something bothering you?"

Gwen frowned down at the table. "Something about Mr. Thorne's journals are strange—not that his wife's aren't as well. But his entries spoke of nothing but love for his wife with only one mention of Miss Wilson. He'd had her at the hall since shortly after his wedding, yet he only mentions her when he says he sent her to town for medicine."

"You sound like you have a theory," he

urged her on. It was fascinating to watch her put the pieces of this old puzzle together.

"I think it's possible that Mrs. Thorne killed Miss Wilson out of jealousy and also fear," she said slowly. "Her entries become increasingly disturbing, saying that she believes someone or something is watching her. She imagined Miss Wilson was skulking around the hallways, trying to take Mr. Thorne from her."

"Poor woman," Robert said quietly.

"There's more to it," Gwen said. "I also think it's possible that Mr. Thorne might have covered for the murder. I've also started to wonder if Mr. Thorne had something to do with her illness." She paused and swallowed hard, looking into his eyes. "Robert," she whispered. "I've heard the moaning...this morning."

He immediately went to her and folded his arms around her to find that she was trembling. "Gwen, dearest."

"I thought it'd stopped," she said into his chest. "I truly thought it had."

Rubbing his hand down her back, he said, "Look, we've both been working hard all day. A bit of dinner will do us both some good. Let me brew a pot of weak tea and see if I can't find something cold in the larder."

Though he tried to pull way from her, she clung to him. "You do believe me, don't you, Robert?"

"Of course," he said tilting up her chin. "No question. If you say it's so, then I believe it." Lightly he brushed his lips against hers. "Now let me see to our dinner."

As he rummaged in the dry larder where he'd found the bread, he heard Gwen at the scullery sink washing dishes. By the time he found a cured ham and a round of cheddar cheese, she'd laid the dining table with plates, cutlery and fresh linen, and also lit the candles. They sat together at the corner, as usual, but he let his foot stray to keep in touch with hers.

As they ate, he regaled her with tales of wheelbarrows and haystacks. To his relief, her mood improved and she seemed her old self. Tomorrow he vowed he would get her into the gardens.

"Though we may not have any dessert,"

Robert said, pushing away his empty plate, "I imagine I can uncork a sweet wine."

"Wine is not the sweetness that I'm thinking of," she said, smiling a little as she looked into his eyes and reached for his hand.

Just the thought of what awaited them upstairs had his shaft swelling again. He grinned at her and raised her hand to his lips. "The papers that my father's steward sent," he murmured against her soft skin, "I must at least assure myself that nothing needs my immediate attention." He gazed at her, the candlelight shimmering in her eyes. "Once that is done, I can assure you that wine will be the last thing on my mind."

## CHAPTER 12

Gwen got into her bed in her sleeping shift, pulled the blankets up over her, and waited for Robert. It was a strange feeling, waiting for him in her bed. Her heart raced at the thought of seeing him, of feeling him beside her, on top of her, and in her. It was exciting and wanton but also not a little frustrating as she listened for his footsteps.

His bundle of papers had been thick, but he'd said he would only attend to something important. She found herself rubbing the back of her hand where he'd kissed it, even as she replayed his words in her mind. Perhaps something had required his immediate action after all.

As the minutes ticked slowly by, she

started to wonder if he'd sought his own chamber. Had he changed his mind? But no, if he'd gone to his own bed chamber, she would have heard him pass by. Perhaps she should go check to see where he was, but the sheets were only now becoming warm. She stretched and tried to stifle a yawn. When had she become so sleepy?

She woke with a sudden start and saw immediately that she was still alone. How long she'd been asleep she couldn't tell, but as she sat up, a strange, faint scent tickled her nose.

Quickly she donned her dressing gown and went out into the hall. She smelled smoke.

"Fire," she gasped. Something downstairs was on fire. "Fire!" she screamed as she dashed down the steps. "Fire! Robert, where are you?"

At the bottom of the stairs, she could see that smoke was coming from his library. "Robert," she screamed as she flew through the open doorway.

He was slouched in his chair, head dangling off to the side. The curtains at the window behind him were on fire.

"Miss!" Parks yelled behind her.

"Parks, thank God!" She pointed behind him. "Bring the fire buckets from the living room hearth."

As the flames crept along the floor, Gwen ran to Robert. She screamed his name and shook him as hard as she could. "Wake up," she pleaded. "Please, Robert!"

Though he stirred, he didn't wake.

Parks dashed past her and flung the sand on the floor and then on the curtains, while she tugged Robert out of his chair and onto the rug in front of it. Grasping him under the shoulders, she hauled him backward with her. He was much heavier than she thought he would be, but every muscle in her body strained to pull him to safety. With each laborious tug, she gained another precious inch.

When she spared a glance for the fire, all she could see was smoke. Had Parks managed to put it out? As if in answer to her question, he emerged from the thick cloud, coughing, only to run past her to the kitchens. He must be going to get water, she thought, tugging Robert's leaden body along the ground. The fire must still be burning. It occurred to her then that she might have to drag him out of the house. Though her back ached, she redoubled her effort.

"Gwen?" she heard Robert murmur, but his voice was thick and the words slurred. "What is happening?"

*"Thank God you're alive,"* she gasped, panting hard, still dragging him slowly to the door.

Parks ran past again, with two pails of water. She heard the hiss of them hitting the fire and the sound of him stamping. But after a minute, he was at her side.

"Is the fire out?" she gasped.

"Yes," Parks choked out. "But we must escape this smoke." Coughing, he grasped the lapels of Robert's coat and quickly dragged him into the hallway.

Finally, well clear of the library, he let Robert back down and Gwen fell to her knees beside him. His eyes were closed and he had still not moved.

"Robert," she tried again, *"please wake up."*

"Hmmm?" she heard him murmur and

his eyebrows lifted, though his eyes remained shut. "Is that you Gwen?"

Why was his speech slurred? How could she rouse him? As a thought occurred to her, she whispered a brief apology, then slapped his face with the full force of her open hand.

"What?" he exclaimed, as his eyes flew open. They finally focused on her. "Gwen? What are you–" He saw Parks on his other side, and then his nostrils flared. "Fire," he said, struggling to sit up. "There's a fire."

"I've put it out, master," Parks said, helping him.

Relief surged through her. "It was in your library, Robert," Gwen told him. "We only just managed to rescue you."

"Rescue me?" he muttered and shook his head as if to clear it. His voice was sounding more firm. "Yes. I heard you but I couldn't rouse myself. It felt as if all of my limbs were made of lead."

Parks exchanged a look with her, before addressing Robert. "Perhaps too much whiskey, sir?"

"I had no whiskey," Robert said, his

words less slurred, but still not right. "Help me up."

As he leaned on them, they helped him to stand. But it was clear he couldn't stay upright without their help.

"All right," Gwen said. "Parks, help me get Mr. Sheraton to his bed. Then you must go for the doctor." Both of them took one of his arms around their shoulders.

"Doctor?" Robert said, as they helped him up the stairs. "Doctor?"

"Yes, Robert," Gwen said, panting again with the effort of supporting him. "I think you've been given some sort of drug."

* * *

DR. THACKERY HAD COME, huffing and puffing, in the small hours of the night. Gwen quickly introduced herself before leading him upstairs.

"Parks tells me you suspect a drug," the older man said, not bothering to take off his coat.

"Yes, doctor," she said, as they climbed. "Despite the fact that his library was on fire, he was very difficult to rouse."

"Right," he said as they reached the top. "Parks told me what happened."

Robert lay on his bed where she and Parks had lain him. Though he was conscious, he was still drowsy and slow of movement. The doctor set his bag down on the bed and threw off his coat.

"Mr. Sheraton," he said, loudly, "do you know who I am?"

"Dr. Thackery," Robert responded. "Don't be ridiculous."

Gwen had to smile a little. The last few hours had been harrowing. As she'd sat by his bedside, she'd watched for even the smallest indication that he might be fading. But his breathing had never faltered and he'd alternately woken and fallen asleep.

"Bring me that candle," he ordered Gwen, pointing at it.

As she brought it to him, Thackery didn't take it but leaned over Robert and motioned her to come closer. With a deft and practiced movement, the doctor thumbed Robert's right eye open wide. Then he did the same to the left.

"Mmm hmm," he said nodding.

"What is it?" Gwen asked.

Ignoring her, he said to Robert, "Open your mouth and stick out your tongue." As the doctor examined it, Gwen was relieved to see that it looked normal—at least she thought it did.

As the doctor straightened, he shooed her back. "Out of my way." He opened his bag and took out a stethoscope. Placing the earpieces in his ears, he put the listening end under Robert's shirt and stood still, seeming to concentrate. "Mmm hmm," he muttered again.

Gwen rolled her eyes, almost beyond patience with the man. Why could he not just tell her his findings?

"Send for Parks," he told her.

Quickly she set the candle back down on the nightstand and raced out the door—and nearly collided with the valet.

"Yes, Miss," he said a bit sheepishly. "I heard the doctor."

"And I hear you," Thackery called to him. "Fetch me a bottle of brandy." She and Parks exchanged puzzled looks. "Make sure it's unopened," Thackery added, more loudly. "And bring a glass."

When Gwen returned to the bed,

Robert had closed his eyes again and the doctor was rummaging in his leather bag. From it he withdrew a dark brown bottle that rattled with the sound of tablets within.

Obviously the man knew something, or at least suspected it. She could no longer contain herself. "Doctor, please, do you have any idea what has happened?"

He paused, scowling his reproach at her. "Well you said it yourself, didn't you? He's been drugged, or more precisely, sedated."

Parks' footsteps pounded up the steps but slowed to a walk as he entered the room, breathing hard. "Brandy, doctor."

"Inspect the seal," he told Gwen then motioned to Parks. "Give me the glass."

Gwen took the bottle and examined the round cork and the thin strip of paper glued to it. Both appeared to be in perfect condition and untouched. "I don't believe it's ever been opened."

The doctor nodded and held out his hand for it. He wasted no time in opening the bottle, looking down inside, and then sniffing it. "Mmm hmm," he said, and then poured a little in the glass. As Gwen watched, she realized that the glass held some sort of crystals, not tablets.

He roused Robert and held the glass to his lips. "Drink this," he ordered. "All of it." As Robert opened his mouth, the doctor expertly tipped the contents of the glass in. "*Swallow*."

As Robert obeyed, his eyes opened wide and he coughed, sputtering. "What in God's name?" He sat up and wiped his mouth on the back of his hand.

Gwen went to his side. "Robert, be careful. Let me–"

"Let him be," the doctor said, as Robert coughed again. Thackery seemed to take no notice but instead added more crystals from the bottle and then some brandy. This time he handed him the glass.

"Again," he said. "All of it."

Though Robert gave him a baleful glare, he did as he was told, followed by another round of coughing. But when he could catch his breath, he said, "What is this vile concoction?"

"Ammonium carbonate," Thackery said, replacing the bottle's stopper. He glanced at all of them, and apparently seeing their confusion added, "Smelling salts."

"Smelling salts?" Robert barked and put a hand to his throat. To Gwen's astonishment—and great relief—he swung his legs over the side of the bed. "Are you trying to poison me?"

"Oh quite to the contrary," the doctor assured him and fixed his gaze on Gwen. "He was indeed sedated. You were quite right to call for me. He'll be fine now."

Her aching shoulders sagged at his reassurance.

"I don't understand," Robert said, setting the glass down with a look of revulsion. "How does drinking smelling salts, of all things, help?"

"Ammonia counteracts the laurel water," the doctor said simply, as if everyone should know that fact.

"Laurel water, sir?" Parks asked. "Begging your pardon, doctor, but how do you know it was laurel water?"

"The smell on Mr. Sheraton's breath," the doctor said, packing his bag. "It was almonds."

"The port," Robert whispered. He

looked at Gwen. "While I was examining my father's papers I poured a glass of port. I only took one sip." He looked at the doctor. "It tasted...off."

The doctor snorted as he put on his coat. "I don't doubt it."

"Do we keep this laurel water in the hall?" Gwen asked, looking between Parks and Robert.

The valet nodded. "Cherry laurel water for coughs and insomnia. It's in the medical closet."

The doctor picked up his bag and gave Robert a long look. "I cannot prove that you were sedated, Mr. Sheraton, not without proper tests. But I would stake my reputation on it." He headed toward the door. "Parks, fetch my rig."

"Wait," Gwen said, hurrying after him. "Dr. Thackery, do you know who treated Mrs. Thorne?"

The doctor frowned, looking from her back to Robert. "What do you mean?"

"Mrs. Thorne," Gwen said, "the wife of the original owner of the hall. I believe she fell ill and died. What did she die from?"

The doctor looked positively baffled.

"The original owner of Dredthorne? I can assure you, Miss Archer, that despite my appearances, the founding of the hall was well before my time." He took out his pocket watch. "Speaking of which, the hour is late and I have another appointment."

"Thank you, doctor," Robert said to Thackery's back. "Send your bill directly."

The doctor snorted. "You can be sure of it."

Keeping one hand on the bed, Robert slowly stood. Gwen went to him and immediately found herself wrapped in his embrace. "Gwen," he whispered into her hair. "Are you all right?"

"I am now," she said, hugging him fiercely, and the tension in her body finally released. Her eyes burning, she buried her face in his chest and quietly began to cry.

Robert's hand stroked her back as he said, "My poor, Gwen. It's been awful for you. You must be exhausted." She could only nod. "I have you to thank for my life," he said quietly.

"And Parks," she said with a sniff. "It took us both to pull you out of the library." She paused and pulled back to look up at him. "Oh, your father's papers. I don't know if–"

He pulled her back against his warm broad chest—not that she resisted for a moment. "The documents will wait," he said. "Sleep will not. Let me close the door."

As he did, she removed her dressing gown. It seemed like a lifetime ago when she'd put it on in her room. He peeled back the covers for her and she gratefully slid in, the sheets still warm from his body lying on top. He snuffed out the candle, and she heard him disrobe.

The same excitement that she'd felt when she'd waited for him in her bed returned, but the weariness of worry and exertion had sunk deep into her bones. When he got into bed, she instantly tucked herself against his side. As he wrapped his arm around her, she sighed deeply and smiled against his smooth skin, and then sleep claimed her before she could draw her next breath.

## CHAPTER 13

*A*s Gwen slowly opened her eyes, she almost had to squint. The morning sun had risen high above the horizon, its bright light spreading across the silk bed covering, over the wool rug, as it filled the room. She stretched, her muscles aching from the exertion of the previous night—not exactly the kind of exertion she'd been planning. Though the evening had been far from what she'd envisioned, today was a new day. A mischievous smile crept over her face as she rolled over, but her smile disappeared when she found the bed empty.

She pushed herself upright and scanned about. The bedchamber was empty as well. "Robert?"

He poked his head out of the dressing room. "Gwen, you're awake." His smile was radiant and his dark eyes sparkled, particularly in the warm sunlight. "Good morning."

A sigh of relief escaped her. "Good morning."

"I have the distinct feeling it's going to be a good day," he said, still looking at her from the dressing room. She realized with some disappointment that he was already dressed.

She smiled a little quizzically at him before patting the bed next to her. "I'm sure you're right," she replied, but to her consternation, he didn't move.

Instead, he waggled his eyebrows and said, "I've found something." Then he disappeared again into the dressing room.

Found something? What could he have possibly found in—

Gwen's heart leapt to her throat as she threw the bedding aside and jumped to the floor. She only remembered to grab her dressing gown at the last moment.

"What is it?" she said breathless, joining him in the small room.

"Look for yourself," he said, pointing with a pen knife. There was something stuck in the wood of the wall's paneling. "If you stand aside, the sunlight will come in."

As she did so, the object there positively glinted. "It couldn't be a nail, could it? Perhaps one that's bent on its side? It's so shiny."

"We're going to find out," he said, his voice as excited as she felt. "But I had to fetch the pen knife. Whatever it is, it's wedged in tightly."

Using the tip of the small blade, he began to chip away at the wood paneling around the object. She waited in suspense as he worked the knife in a tiny circle around it, moving so carefully he might have been a surgeon. As she watched, the tiny wood splinters fell to the floor, and a vague, if rough, outline began to form. She had not been far off the mark when she thought it might be a nail bent on its side. Finally he began to dig beneath it, using the blade as a lever. With a small pop, the shiny object sprang from the wall and landed on the floor at her feet.

She picked it up. "Why, it's an earring," she said, astonished.

Though the hook had been lost, there was no doubt it was an earring. It would have dangled from the ear, long and incredibly ornate. Perhaps two dozen small, circular stones were arranged in what appeared to be a cascade of flowers. She held it up to the sun, watching as small rainbows danced inside them. Now she could see that most of the stones were crystal clear, but some had yellowish and pink castes.

"Heavens," she said. "I do believe these might be diamonds." She laid it in his outstretched hand.

After a few moments examining it, he looked up at her grinning. "I believe you're right. It is a diamond earring, and a rather elaborate one." He glanced over his shoulder at the small divot he'd left in the paneling. "The question then becomes, how on earth did it get there?"

"And who did it belong to?" she added as a new dread settled in her chest. "Robert, someone tried to kill you last night. I think the owner of this earring, whoever it may be, could be responsible."

"Really?" He folded the knife closed and pocketed it. "I don't see the connection."

"Honestly," she admitted. "I don't either. It's just a feeling I have. Perhaps something that I've read in the journals."

He also pocketed the tiny piece of jewelry in his waistcoat. "Thackery said I was sedated. If someone had wanted me dead, why not poison me?"

She frowned at him. "You're splitting hairs. It's only a matter of degrees. Who can say what would have happened if you'd drunk more?"

"The fire could have been an accident," he countered. "Started by a candle I might have knocked over."

Now he was starting to make her angry. "Then we shall go down to the library and see."

* * *

BY THE TIME they went to the library, Parks had almost finished cleaning it. Robert did his best to disguise his disappointment at his valet's prompt and fastidious action.

"Your papers appear in good order, sir," the valet said, indicating the bundle.

"Good," Robert said and exchanged a look with an obviously displeased Gwen.

"I'm afraid I won't be able to save the curtains, sir." He indicated the charred pile of fabric on the floor. A strong smell of smoke emanated from them. Then he pointed at the ceiling. "I'll have to fetch the ladder to clean the ceiling."

A ring of black soot stained the ornate panels above them.

"Parks," Gwen interjected, "did you find a candle overturned, perhaps on the floor, that might have started the fire?"

"No, Miss," Parks replied. "There was nothing on the floor."

Gwen smiled primly as she looked at Robert and nodded.

"You're certain?" Robert said as he walked over to where the fire had obviously singed the floorboards. It'd then crept up the curtains and almost set the ceiling on fire, its destructive path only too clear.

Parks looked from Robert to Gwen and then back again. "Absolutely certain, sir."

Gwen moved to the desk where the bundle of papers still sat, where Robert had left them, but then she cocked her head and turned to face them.

"And the port?" Gwen asked, looking around the room. "What has happened to it?"

"Well, Miss," Parks said quickly, "after what the doctor said, I thought I'd better pour it down the sink. So that's what I did." He glanced nervously at Robert. "Did I do right, sir?"

"Yes, of course, Parks," Robert said in a soothing voice. "Miss Archer and I are just reviewing the...facts, as it were."

"I presume you've also washed the glass," Gwen said, more statement than question.

"Yes, Miss," his valet said, grimacing. "But that's all. I swear it. That's all that I've removed."

Before his valet could feel any worse for doing his job, Robert said, "That will be all, Parks. I appreciate your cleaning up. Thank you."

With another worried look at Gwen, Parks bowed to them both and hurriedly went to the door.

"Oh, and Parks?" Robert added. His valet turned back to him. "Thank you for helping to save my life last night."

A smile lit the older man's face. "Yes, sir. Of course, sir." He bowed and left.

When Gwen turned to him, Robert expected that her consternation might overflow. But instead a devious little grin curled her lips. "Do you see what is missing?"

As Robert turned about the room, he tried to picture it as it was last night. He'd brought in the bottle of port and a glass, and then remembered that he'd left the bundle of papers in the secret library. He'd brought them here to the desk and untied the string that bound them. Then he'd struck a match, and lit the candle in its holder.

"The candle," he muttered, scanning the entire room.

Gwen came to stand at his side. "Strange isn't it? That the one thing that could have started the fire is completely missing, let alone on the floor?"

"Well, it has to be here," he said, moving aside the papers and the inkstand. "Parks said that the port and glass were all that he removed." But the more he looked, the more it seemed she was right. Though he searched the myriad bookshelves, the various small tables, and even moved the urns and sculptures set upon them, the candle and holder were nowhere to be seen. He turned to Gwen, somewhat chastened.

"You're right," he said. "It isn't here."

Her eyes took on a twinkle. "There is one more thing for which we can search." Luckily she didn't wait for him to guess. "A secret passage."

He drew his brows together. "I've been in and out of this room a hundred times, Gwen." When he saw her face fall, he stopped himself. "All right, what makes you think we'd find one here?"

"The missing candle," she said, smiling. With hands on her hips, she surveyed the entire room. "We must turn this place upside down and inside out if that's what it takes. But I'm telling you, there's more hidden in Dredthorne Hall than we have glimpsed. Mrs. Thorne sensed it even if she couldn't say it in so many words. She wrote repeatedly that Miss Wilson moved in the shadows."

Robert took off his jacket, tossed it on a chair, and rolled up the sleeves of his shirt. "Where shall we start?"

Now she beamed at him. "I adore it when you let me have my way," she said, then put a finger to her chin as she considered. After a moment, she gave a reproving tsk. "Of course. We must start near the fire."

As she directed, he moved the ruined curtains aside and she stepped to the wall. "In my dressing room, there was a distinct if very thin line where the wall was divided."

"Yes," he said, joining her in front of the flocked paper-hanging that covered the wall. Though it was fire-darkened, it was otherwise undamaged. "I recall how it looked in the kitchen as well. But in an old building like this, such small cracks wouldn't be out of place."

"And difficult to see," she agreed, "if you didn't know to look. But perhaps..." She smoothed her fingers across the wall. "...it would be easier to feel than see." She closed her eyes.

Though he knew that he should do the same, he couldn't help but watch her for a moment. A tiny furrow creased the space between her elegant eyebrows as she concentrated. Her petal shaped lips parted, ever so slightly, and he could see her eyes moving beneath the closed lids.

"Your staring at me isn't going to help," she said quietly, eyes still closed. A little smile played across her lips. "Try the other wall."

Reluctantly he left her and began his own touch exploration. Because of the deeply textured flocking, it was as difficult to feel a fine detail as it was to see it. For several silent minutes, the two of them explored. But just when he'd been ready to give up, his index finger brushed over something. He stopped and opened his eyes.

At first he didn't see anything, amidst the mass of swirling designs meant to look like cut velvet flowers and leaves. But just to the left of his finger, there was something he couldn't quite make out. Was it a shadow? He moved closer for a better look. No, it was a gap—and a straight one at that. His gaze shot downward, following the line all the way to the floor.

"Gwen? I think you should have a look at this."

She was at his side in an instant. "You did it!" she exclaimed. "Now push, just to one side of the line."

Again he did as she instructed, and they were instantly rewarded with a small click, the sound of faint scraping, and the revolving door moving inward.

"Amazing," he whispered, as they peered inside.

Dust and cobwebs filled the short passage which ended in a sharp left turn. Beyond that, there was only darkness.

"It needs light," she said, hurrying off and returning with two candles and matches. He quickly lit them and, when she would have gone first, he put a light hand on her shoulder to restrain her. "Honestly," she said, "I explored the first one on my own."

"That's because I wasn't there," he said, "and you were more foolhardy then. Now that you are mine, I cannot permit it." Then he pointed at the floor just inside the door. "Besides, look at what you would have tread on."

There, in the dust of the floor, were scuff marks. She lowered her candle to them. "If I'm not mistaken, these are fresh. No dust has settled within them."

"Can you tell if they are from a man or woman's shoe?" he asked, since the narrow passage would only fit one of them.

She shook her head and stood. "They're just scuff marks."

Though she looked into the passage, lifting her candle for what light it shed, she did not proceed further. Instead, with a heavy sigh, she stayed where she was. Finally she looked at him, and motioned for him to pass her.

\* \* \*

AS GWEN FOLLOWED Robert into the dark

passage, and made the left turn, she could barely suppress her excitement. Where would it lead? Would they find a secret room at last? Had Mrs. Thorne been right about Miss Wilson skulking in deep shadows?

Although this passageway was of a height where they didn't need to crawl, it wound left and right so many times that she completely lost her sense of direction. Where in the world could they possibly be after so many steps?

Robert came to a stop in front of her. "There it is," he finally said.

"Do you see the end?" she gasped, hopping and trying to look over his rather broad and too tall shoulder.

"It's a pit of darkness," he said. "So I suspect so." In another moment, they had their answer. "I believe it's another revolving door."

"Open it," she said eagerly. "Let's go through."

He glanced over his shoulder and caught her eye. "Be prepared to run, Gwen. If I say the word, I want you to turn on your heel and run as fast as your legs will take you." He paused until she nodded. "Good. Now stand back."

She backed up two paces and held her candle high.

"Here we go," he muttered as he pushed on the door.

Light spilled around them as the revolving door slowly spun. Robert stepped through, still blocking the exit, as he quickly checked left and right. Finally he stood aside and motioned her through.

She emerged into a large room, though somewhat barren and undecorated. It held a simple, long wooden table, with at least a dozen well-used chairs on each side of it. Two moderately better chairs sat at each end. There were two exits, though both doors were closed, and a small fireplace was located in the corner, unused.

Because there were no windows, she couldn't even use the grounds to orient herself. "I don't recognize this place," she said, gazing around at it.

"You wouldn't," Robert said. "It's the servant's hall."

"The servant's hall," she echoed, lifting her candle. Then her eyes widened. "Oh heavens. Servants?" When she looked at him, her brows had arched high. "Parks is–"

"Beyond reproach," Robert declared. "The man has been serving the Sheraton family for his entire adult life. Also, I might remind you, he's the only one who stayed."

"Well that's just it, isn't it?" she said. "He's the only one here besides us."

"And your ghosts," he reminded her, and then grimaced. He paused and took a deep breath. "Look, I don't know about you, but I'm starving. Let's have something to eat. I'll think better when my stomach isn't hollow."

Though she wasn't convinced at the sudden change in conversation, she thought better of pressing her point. "I'm famished," she said, and looked at both exits. "Which way are the kitchens?"

## CHAPTER 14

*A*lthough their meal consisted of cold cured ham, cheddar cheese and bread again, Gwen wouldn't complain. It'd been a stellar day so far. She'd managed to convince Robert that indeed someone had set the fire, and then likely taken the candle with them through the new secret passage. Though she'd probably never convince him that it could have been Parks, that fact seemed obvious to her. But what she couldn't puzzle out was why. What would the valet have to gain? If he wanted to steal, there was every opportunity. Certainly he could never inherit.

Inheritance, she thought. There was something about that notion that bothered her. She took another bite of her ham before it occurred to her.

"Robert, do you still have that earring?" He seemed lost in thought and she realized that, while she'd eaten nearly all her food, most of his was untouched. "Robert?"

"What?" he said, looking at her. "Oh yes, of course." He produced it from his waistcoat pocket. "Here it is."

She examined the exquisite jewelry in a new light, particularly the different colored diamonds. She was quite sure her conclusion was right. "It belonged to Miss Wilson."

He stared at her, a dumbfounded look on his face. "How could you possibly know that?"

"Too many diamonds," she said. "Look at it. It's not just an earring, it's a statement. Remember that there must have been another one to match it as well, and likely some sort of necklace or pendant too." She set it on the table between them. "Mrs. Thorne impresses me as a more serious woman. Not only that, she had all of this." She looked around the living room. "She had Dredthorne Hall and possibly an inheritance or dowry of her own. But a courtesan who lived on the kindness of her paramours? This would be her only support, her only form of security."

He regarded her solemnly. "One can hardly refute your logic, dear Gwen." But when she thought he might take her hand, or congratulate her, he looked back at his plate.

"So," she said in a teasing tone, trying to lighten his mood, "it would seem you've had a courtesan in your bedchamber, Mr. Sheraton. Would you care to explain?"

He set down his fork and knife. "I'm sorry, Gwen. I'm afraid you must leave."

If he'd told her that the moon was made of green cheese, she couldn't have been more thunderstruck. "I don't understand," was all she could think to say.

"I should have made you leave when Frances died, or when my chair legs were sawed through, or when the chandelier fell. Now we find that this damnable hall could be riddled through with secret passages. I cannot safeguard you under these circumstances. So I must ask you to leave."

"But after everything we've been

through together," she said, trying to keep the pleading tone out of her voice, but not succeeding. "After everything we mean to each other. How can you–"

"That is precisely why, my dearest Gwen." He took her hand in both of his. "I cannot in good conscience keep you with me, though I desire it more than anything in the world."

She took her hand back. "Well certainly I have some say in it," she declared. "I am not to be–"

"No, Gwen," he said, standing. "You do not have a say in it. Please pack your trunks. I'll let Parks know."

With that he stalked off, and Gwen knew from the stiff set of his shoulders and his pounding footsteps, that he meant every word. More than that, she knew he would not be moved by anything she could say—because he was right.

## CHAPTER 15

*W*hen Gwen came down the stairs in her heavy traveling coat and bonnet, Robert was waiting for her.

"Are you ready?" he asked quietly.

"Everything is packed," she said curtly, without looking at him.

Though she tried to pass him by as she headed to the entry hall, he caught her arm. "Gwen, please," he said. "This is the last thing I want. Surely you must know that." He turned her to face him. "I'd give anything to have you with me."

"Then let me stay," she blurted out, glaring into his chest. "I can take care of myself. I can–"

He lifted her chin and the moment that

she'd dreaded was upon her. His soft gaze lingered on her eyes, then her lips, and the resolve that she'd spent the last hour hoarding evaporated.

"Oh, Robert," she sighed, her eyes filling with tears as she fell into his arms.

"I know," he whispered. "I feel just the same."

For a long time he simply held her, and Gwen prayed it could go on forever. No place felt safer than in his strong arms and nestled against his hard chest. But when he finally drew back, he didn't let her go. Instead he held her face between his wonderful hands, and leaned down and kissed her. Unlike their first kiss, there was no hurry and no crush. Instead, he took his time as he melded their lips together. His mouth was warm and gentle, and his touch so full of tenderness that she felt she could cry again. With the soft and insistent caress of his lips, he kissed her breathless and when they finally separated, she had to gasp.

"Don't forget that," he whispered and touched his forehead to hers. "Because I won't."

She smiled through her tears. "I couldn't if I tried."

He let her go and stood back, then gazed through the open entry. "Where is Parks? I'll need his help with those trunks."

She swiped at her eyes and sniffed a little. "Perhaps he needs help with the rig?"

"I'll go and find out," he said.

Quickly, she latched onto his arm. She'd spend every last second that she could with him. "I'll go with you."

The day outside was gray with a dense fog that blanketed the grounds and surrounding land. Though the mist was heavy, the temperature wasn't as severely cold as it had been. Riding in the rig wouldn't be freezing, but it would be wet.

"I'm sending Parks with you," he said. "He'll purchase a carriage and horse for us in Renwick, if he can find one. Even a pony cart would do. Just something to–"

As they crossed the threshold of the stable, they saw a body on the ground.

Robert surged forward, as Gwen lifted her skirts and coat and ran after him. Her hand flew to her mouth and she gasped. It was Parks, laying on his back.

"Oh, Robert! Is he…?"

Robert pressed his fingers to the valet's neck. She saw a gash on the older man's forehead and bruising on his cheek. "No, he's alive, but his pulse is very weak."

"Oh, thank God, he's not dead."

Robert hesitated, holding his valet's hand lightly. It was the first time that she could recall Robert looking indecisive. She fidgeted, looking at the hall over her shoulder. Suddenly, the stately building looked more than imposing; its shutters looked like gashes against the exterior as if torn by a knife. The doors were deep, black holes from which no one would return.

"It's growing dark," he finally said, standing. "We can take him into the house, but he may not see out the night." He looked down at Parks. "He needs a doctor." Then Robert looked at her. "Gwen, I think we need to take him to Renwick."

"In the dark," she said flatly. They both understood. Not only would there be no moon to steer by in the fog, but highwaymen would surely be laying in wait along the roads.

He stripped off his coat and layed it

over Parks' chest. "I'm going to retrieve my pistols," he said. "Are you up to this? I can't leave you here alone."

"I'm with you, Robert," she said decisively. "Hall or highway."

"Good girl," he said, taking her hand. "Is there a small case that you want to bring with you?" She nodded. "Then let's go."

Hand in hand they ran back to the hall. "The pistols are in the library," he said. "Stay with me, then we'll get your case and leave."

But as they dashed into the library, they skidded to a sudden halt. The pistols were indeed there—in Christopher's hands.

GWEN'S KNEES shook so hard that her skirts rustled. The only thing more shocking than seeing Christopher at Dredthorne was seeing Regina bound and gagged, kneeling at his feet.

"*Regina*," Gwen breathed.

Thick rope bound her arms and legs, trussed up like an animal. Her auburn hair was wild and knotted, her mouth hidden by a thick gag. Tears streamed down her face as she whimpered, green eyes wide, staring at Gwen.

"Hello, brother," Christopher said mildly. He gestured with one of the pistols to the sofa. "Do take a seat, both of you."

Though Gwen took half a step toward Regina, Robert took her arm and firmly moved her toward the sofa.

"A wise course," Christopher agreed, smiling pleasantly, as they sat down.

Gwen barely heard his words, not able to take her eyes off her sister. She was terribly thin and her eyes were swollen as if she'd cried for a month. Despite the guns pointed at her and Robert, a seething, blind anger began to rage inside her.

"So, brother, how do you fare?" Christopher said. "Evidently very well, considering all of the effort I've put into killing you. You are a remarkably hardy fellow."

Gwen clenched her jaw and heard her teeth grind. So here was the true ghost of Dredthorne. Here was the source of all their fear and worry.

Christopher was a smaller and softer

echo of his brother. Though he'd always impressed her as a handsome dandy, his brown mop of hair was tousled now, and dark stubble coated his jaw.

"Thank you, brother," Robert replied, keeping his tone light. "You've played quite the game."

Christopher tossed his head back and laughed. An image of him as that spirited young man she'd known all those years ago flashed into her mind. What had happened to him?

"Indeed," Christopher said as his laughter trailed off. "I always was better at games, you know." He suddenly sobered and cleared his throat. "Most games, at any rate."

Gwen couldn't take this idle chatter another moment. "Why do you want us to die, Christopher?" she said in a voice that shook with anger as much as fear.

Christopher snorted. "You? You're merely a secondary casualty, Gwen," he said flatly. "I honestly wasn't expecting you to stay, let alone fall in love with my discourteous brother. Though I must say it was rather amusing to hear you carry on about ghosts and journals and such. You have such a lively imagination."

"Why?" was all Robert said, but the one word spoke much more. It seemed to reverberate in the air between them.

"Do try to understand, Robert," his brother said, growing earnest for the first time. "You see, I'm in a rather large amount of debt."

"This is for money?" Gwen demanded, her tone harsh. Robert squeezed her hand.

"No, you idiot," Christopher spat at her. "He has to die so that I may inherit —*everything.*" He turned a cold and lethal look on his brother. "Robert, the serious. Robert, the responsible. Robert, the heir of the Sheraton estate."

"You could have gone to father," Robert told him. "He loved you. You could have come to me as well."

Christopher laughed again, but this time Gwen heard a tinge of mania in it. "And now you'd be Robert, the charitable. Does it never end? Why must I beg for your indulgence?" He waved the pistols erratically and Gwen couldn't help but flinch. "Because I had the great misfortune of being born the second son, that's why."

"Christopher," Robert began, "you are still my brother. Whatever you need–"

Still gripping the pistol, Christopher turned the weapon to show him his hand. Gwen gasped. The smallest and ring finger were missing, down to the knuckle.

"It's a bit late for my hand," he declared. He looked from his brother to her and back again. "Oh, I see. You've never had a gambling debt."

"Gambling?" Robert said.

"How I love my games," Christopher said, without an ounce of mirth. "And how they love me." For the first time, he glanced down at Regina. "I was on top of the world. I was going to give her everything."

Regina looked at him, wide-eyed, and shook her head violently.

"Oh, shut up," Christopher said absently. He turned his attention back to Robert. "So you see, dear brother, I shall take control of the Sheraton estate. There'll be enough for my debts, and more besides, if I sell all of the family's interests." He gazed around the room. "Including this dreadful place."

Gwen's stomach clenched as she realized there was no reasoning with him. This was not the Christopher of their youth. This was some madman who held them at gunpoint. Robert must have realized it too.

"Let the women go," he said calmly to his brother. "They've done nothing to deserve this."

"Oh please," Christopher sneered. "Robert, the chivalrous. Do you really think I'd trust two women not to tell a soul?" Then he grinned at his brother, his eyes shining. "But not to worry, dear brother, I shall wait until you are dead."

"But you love Regina," Gwen protested. "You were going to give her everything."

Christopher shook his head, tsking. "Until she rejected me. Naturally I told my future bride everything. It would have been so much easier with her help." He looked down at her as though he were deeply disappointed. "The poor thing was beside herself, really."

A thought occurred to Gwen, and

despite their dire circumstances, she had to know. "Regina has been here the entire time?"

"Of course," Christopher said, matter-of-factly. "I could hardly let her run about the countryside."

Gwen looked at Robert, his expression as grim as she felt. "The whimpering, the sobbing," she said. "It wasn't Miss Wilson. It was Regina that I was hearing."

All those times she'd questioned her sanity, the strange things that the servants had heard—it had all been Christopher and her desperate sister. Though Gwen had thought the journals were helping her, they'd only fed her fears.

"And now it is time to end this," Christopher said almost gayly. "Robert, do help Regina up."

## CHAPTER 16

*C*autiously, Robert rose and slowly moved toward Regina. Although he looked down on the kneeling woman, he kept Christopher in his peripheral vision. If he could get a clear path to his brother, he might be able to tackle and subdue him long enough for Gwen to escape with her sister.

"I see how your mind turns, dear brother," Christopher warned him, stepping behind Regina. He pointed a pistol at each of the women. "Do not mistake chivalry for stupidity." He motioned with the pistol. "Up, up. Get her on her feet."

Robert did as he was told, supporting Regina under one arm as he helped her to stand. Though she swayed, he managed to keep her on her feet. She was in a frightful state, and he could only imagine that the tenacity of the Archer women must be formidable to survive under these circumstances—for survive they would. If he had to give his life in order to prevail, he would do it.

"We are going on a trip, brother," Christopher said. "Get up," he snapped at Gwen.

As she slowly rose, she asked, "Where… where are we going?"

"It will be a short trip, just up the stairs." He motioned with a jerk of his head. "We're going to Robert's bedchamber." He leered at her. "I believe you know the way."

With one hand still under Regina's arm, Robert held out a hand to Gwen. "Come," was all he said.

As they exited the library and mounted the first steps, he glanced over his shoulder. Though likely mad, his brother was not foolish, and made sure to stay well back.

"What can we do?" Gwen whispered.

"If I say to run," he said under his breath, "grab your sister and–"

"Tut, tut," Christopher said, and Robert

heard him cock one of the pistols. "There'll be none of that."

They climbed the stairs slowly to allow for Regina's stumbling, wobbly gait. Though Robert watched for his chance to attack his brother, while yet keeping the women safe, there was simply no opportunity. Christopher had been very clever to use two pistols to keep him at bay.

As they walked to the bedroom, Gwen sniffed the air. "What is that smell?"

Robert frowned. There was a familiar scent that he couldn't place, growing stronger as they approached his bedchamber. Gwen clutched his hand. "What is that?" she said, louder this time.

But before Robert could answer, he heard Christopher running, but couldn't turn in time. His brother shoved both pistols in his back and pushed with all his might. Gwen and Regina had no choice but to follow as Gwen clung to him and he supported her sister. Together they careened through the door, toppling onto the floor in a tangle.

Robert immediately tried to push himself up, but his hands pressed into the sopping rug and slipped. He could only watch as Christopher picked up a ready candle next to the door and tossed it on the floor between them.

"No escape this time, brother," Christopher said, stepping quickly backward through the door, before locking it.

Flames leaped from the candle and raced unbelievably fast toward the three of them. Only then did Robert realize what his brother had done.

"Oil," he grunted, as he stood on the slippery mess. "Hurry."

Gwen was already trying to stand, but struggling to help Regina, who was still bound. As the blaze roared to life around them, Robert rushed to them, slipping and sliding. "Gwen," he yelled, as he grabbed Regina's arm, "it's too slippery. You must crawl." He pointed in the one direction that was clear of fire. "That way."

Even as the heat and flames spread behind them, Robert dragged Regina after Gwen and finally off the burning rug. Smoke was beginning to fill the room. Without more air, they wouldn't burn to death, they'd suffocate. But the rug—and the fire—stood between him and the window.

Though his boots still slipped on the floorboards, the more steps he took the better grip they had. He tried in vain to open the locked doorknob and then saw his solution.

"Gwen," he yelled. "Cover Regina!"

He picked up the largest chair in the room, gave himself a quarter spin, and hurled it at the window. Gwen dove over Regina, covering her sister with her body.

With a deafening crash, the shattered pane of glass flew outward with the chair, smoke pouring out with it. Robert dashed to the desk, shoving it off the rug just before the fire reached it. Next came the table and chair as he pulled them off the rug to safety, though they were singed.

"You can't save all the furniture!" Gwen yelled, as she tugged her sister further away from the growing conflagration.

He picked up the edge of the oil soaked rug and rolled it. "I'm not!"

Gwen must have realized his intention as she ran to his side and landed on her knees. Together they folded the burning textile over on itself, then over again.

"Stand back!" he said, as he picked up the rug, hauled it to the window, and shoved it over the edge of the sill.

Far below, he heard the rug land with a thump. In the sudden silence, he gasped for breath and heard Gwen cough. Regina only sobbed.

"Heavens," Gwen said at last, "Regina." She staggered to her feet. "Robert, do you still have your pen knife?"

In short order, Robert cut Regina's bonds as Gwen untied the gag.

"*Sister*," Regina cried, and fell into Gwen's arms.

"Regina, are you all right?" Gwen sobbed. "I thought I would never see you again."

Robert left the two women as they reunited and tried the door again. The knob was old but quite strong and the door itself thick. Short of a key, it wouldn't be opening without a great deal of effort. He next went to the window and looked down. It was far too high to jump, nor were there any handholds that could be used to scale the face of the building. He gazed out into the fog. There had to be a way to get help.

"He forced me to write that awful letter to you," Regina was saying, when he returned to them. She was using her gag to wipe her nose and eyes. "All this time I thought that at any moment he'd kill me. Oh, Gwen, it was horrible. I cried every night."

"I heard you," Gwen said quietly. Tenderly she hugged her sister and rubbed her back, but then she went still. She pulled back and looked at Robert. "What did I say?" She blinked. "I said I heard her!"

"The courtesan," Robert said, stealing a glance to his dressing room. "The earring."

In an instant, they'd both crossed to the small room. "It has to be here," Gwen murmured.

"What does?" Regina asked from the bedchamber. Robert heard her struggle to her feet and come to the door.

"You," Gwen said, even as Robert answered, "A secret door."

Frantically, Gwen moved her fingers across the walls as he did the same. Robert knew from the one they'd found in the library that it wouldn't be easy to find. "We must use a plan and go in order," he said, "or we're sure to miss it."

"I don't think it's on this wall," she said, seeming not to have heard him. She looked at the end of the small room where a cabinet for his clothes stood. "Robert, can you move that clothes press?"

With a great deal of effort, he managed to pull one corner of the heavy furniture away from the wall. Gwen slipped behind it and uttered a quick gasp. "*It's here.*"

"Gwen, wait for me," he called to her. "Let me go first. We don't know where–" But he heard the telltale scrape of the revolving door. "Regina," he said turning back to her. "Can you fetch the candle from next to the bed?"

When she returned with the lit candle, Robert took it from her. "Gwen, you may as well come out so I can go first, because I am not going to give this candle to you."

As he and Regina exchanged a look, a chagrined Gwen finally emerged. "I was going to let you go first." She went to her sister and held her around the shoulders.

Behind the clothes press, the

passageway was the same height as the one they'd found in the library, and equally dark and dirty. But unlike that one, the dust appeared undisturbed.

"I don't think anyone has been in here for some time," Robert said, lifting the candle.

They'd only gone a few yards when the narrow corridor opened up into a small room. But when Robert saw what lay on the floor, he tried to keep the ladies back.

"No, Gwen," he said and tried to block her view, but it was too late.

"Oh no," she whispered.

Robert nodded. "I'm afraid so."

There on the floor was the body—or what used to be the body—of a small woman. Only bones and rotted cloth remained, but she had clearly been wearing a long dress and fine boots. Robert lowered the candle to the body and saw traces of red lace in the clothing. Around the bones of the neck, he saw the soft glow of a string of pearls. In fact, the more he looked, the more tiny glints of jewelry he could see.

"Robert, that earring," Gwen said pointing. "I think it's…"

He picked it up and handed it to her. It was the exact match of the one he'd dug out of the wall. "You were right."

Regina put a shaking hand to her chest. "How can you two be so calm about this? Why are you picking jewelry off a corpse? It's positively hideous."

"I'm sorry, Regina," Gwen said, going to her. "It's just that we are finally meeting Miss Wilson, a courtesan and guest of the original owner of the hall, Mr. Thorne."

"Who?" her sister asked, turning away from the gruesome sight.

"It doesn't matter now," Robert said to them. "We must find an escape so that we don't meet a similar end." Regina quickly nodded her agreement. "Good. Let us proceed then."

Another few yards led them through one turn after another, until finally they reached another revolving door, even though the passageway continued on.

"Where are we?" Gwen whispered.

Robert shook his head and glanced at Regina who did the same. After the turns in the dark, there was no way to know where they were. He put his fingers to his mouth to signal silence and handed the candle to Gwen. Turning back to the door, he pushed at its edge and heard the customary scrape. A shaft of light from the opening spilled across the passage and Robert chanced a quick look. He recognized it immediately. It was Gwen's room. He angled his gaze as far left and right as he could and listened for any sound. It seemed the room was empty. Finally he pushed the door open enough to squeeze through and checked in every direction. Silently he motioned for them to follow.

The sheets were still rumpled from the last time he and Gwen had slept there. Her trunks were waiting where she'd left them. Somehow they had to make it down the stairs and get out of the house and over to the stable—all without coming across his insane and lethally armed brother.

But even as the plan formed in his mind, he heard something in the hallway beyond the open door. Though he dared to hope that it was Parks, recovered from the blow to his head, prudence dictated a different course. He took the pen knife from his pocket and waved the women back. This time, no matter who was out there, Robert had the advantage of surprise. If it was Parks, he could apologize later.

As he silently crept forward, he hid the knife hand behind his back. At the doorway, he took a breath, and charged into the hallway.

But Christopher must have heard him, for his pistols were raised and pointed squarely at Robert's chest. Only steps from where his brother stood at the top of the stairs, Robert came to a stop.

"Oh, Robert," his brother sighed theatrically. "Somehow I knew I had better check. You prove annoyingly resilient." Christopher glanced over Robert's shoulder and for a moment foreboding sank in Robert's stomach. Had Gwen followed him? "Did you leave the ladies to burn?" Christopher asked, grinning. "Now you begin to see that we're not so different."

Apparently Gwen and her sister were still hidden. He forced a smile to his lips. "Exactly, brother," Robert said, in his most reasonable tone. "Now that it's just us two, let's be sensible."

A wild glint lit Christopher's eye. "Oh I am." He raised one of the pistols to take aim, pointed it at Robert's chest, and cocked the hammer.

Robert whipped his arm from behind his back and let the pen knife fly. Twin pistol shots resounded in the air. Ducking low, Robert heard a lead ball smash into the ceiling behind him. Without a weapon now, he would have to charge his brother bare-handed. But when he looked at Christopher, his brother's ashen face was looking down. At the front of his shin a gaping hole had appeared, with blood spurting from it.

"The second pistol," Robert breathed.

Christopher stumbled backward, perhaps attempting to escape, but his leg wouldn't support him. As Robert watched in horror, his brother dropped the pistols and plunged backward. Even as Robert raced to the edge of the stairs, he knew it was too late. His brother landed on his back halfway down the steps, but his momentum sent him further, flipping over and tumbling, until he rolled limply onto the floor, his neck at an impossible angle. Robert raced down the stairs reaching him only moments later, but he watched as the light faded from Christopher's staring eyes.

"*Christopher!*" Regina shrieked from the top of the stairs. She collapsed into her sister's arms, sobbing as Gwen pulled her back from the edge, and the two of them sat down hard on the floor. His eyes met Gwen's, hers full of sympathy and sorrow, before he looked down at his brother.

Finally, it was over.

## CHAPTER 17

*G*wen glanced behind at Regina asleep in the back seat of the rig, and Parks on the floor at her feet. They'd piled almost every blanket they could find on top of the two of them. Robert had taken only a few minutes to reload the pistols before they'd set out for Renwick. She leaned her head on Robert's shoulder as he drove her mare through the darkness.

Robert squeezed her hand lightly, looking grim. He'd put Christopher's body in the library, and covered it with a linen. They had already agreed that he would report a regrettable accident to the police. Christopher had been bringing his gun upstairs to clean, and startled himself when he realized it was loaded. Implausible as it might seem, it ironically fit the facts.

Up ahead a few lights shone through the fog.

"There it is," Gwen gasped. "We've made it."

Gwen directed him through a few streets until Robert stopped the rig in front of the Archer's house. After the opulence of Dredthorne, Gwen was struck by how modest her childhood home was. As she expected, there were no lights on, nor any smoke from the chimney.

After Robert helped her down, she strode up the familiar path and knocked on the door. She heard Regina stirring behind her as Robert informed her that they'd arrived home. Though Gwen had to knock a few more times, a light finally came on in the front room. Her father's weathered face appeared in the window with a candle, and his jaw dropped at what he beheld. Through the door, she could hear him shouting for her mother. Despite the circumstances in which she'd returned, she smiled at the sound of his voice and how it warmed her heart.

Gwen heard the sound of the latch, as Robert and Regina joined her. Then her mother burst through the door.

"Regina!" she exclaimed, throwing her arms around her daughter's neck. "Where have you been? What has happened?"

Gwen found herself wrapped up in her father's fierce hug. "I despaired of seeing either of you again," he said. Then he must have seen Robert. "Mr. Sheraton. Do I have you to thank for this happy reunion?"

Robert bowed to him. "In the end, we three worked together to...affect our outcome." He nodded at the rig in the lane behind him. "But I must beg your forgiveness. I must find a doctor for my valet."

"Your valet?" her father said, concern in his voice. "Well certainly. Let me tell you where you may find him."

As her mother fluttered around Regina and hurried her into the house, and her father escorted Robert to the rig and gave him directions, Gwen hovered on the threshold between the two. Here in the tiny village of Renwick, Dredthorne Hall almost seemed as though it'd been some fantasy, with its journals and secret passages. But Frances and Christopher were both dead, and that had not been a dream. As her father returned to her, Robert accompanied him.

"With your permission, sir," Robert said, "I'd like to bid Miss Archer goodbye."

Though Gwen knew that they would have to part, the word 'goodbye' took her aback. She was not ready to say goodbye—far from it. Nothing that they'd endured had prepared her for this moment.

"Yes, of course," her father said. As he retreated to the house, he gave her a wink and squeezed her shoulder. "Don't stay too long out in the cold."

When the door closed behind her, Robert looked into her eyes, but kept a proper distance between them.

"I must arrange two funerals now," he said. "I shall see to it quickly, but I don't know when I'll see you again."

"I know," she said quietly. "We must do our duties."

He nodded and seemed like he might take her hand, but instead glanced over her shoulder at the house. He cleared his throat. "Well, then, I must–"

"When it's time, we shall go back to Dredthorne together," she declared. "I feel we have a duty there: to Frances, and Miss Wilson, and to ourselves."

Though his face was haggard, and his journey not yet over, his eyes seemed to blaze in the darkness. "I shall hold you to that, Miss Archer." He gave her a bow. "Until then."

\* \* \*

THE SERVICE in London had been simple but dignified, as Robert had instructed the Sheraton's funeral furnisher. Black crepe, muslin, and ostrich feathers had been liberally used throughout, and the procession from the sanctuary to the churchyard had been accompanied by bell ringing. There had been tributes for his father and kind words for his brother—or at least the man that his brother had once been. The Archers had met his mother, and then accompanied her, Robert, and their other relatives to the graveside.

As the clergyman intoned the last words of his prayer, Robert noted how well Regina looked, nearly recovered from her mysterious disappearance. Gwen, of course, was such a vision, even in black, that he had to guard himself from looking at her overly long.

In truth, he'd done his mourning at Dredthorne. Those grim days after his father's death, while he waited in vain for Christopher, had been dark. Though he'd been glad to comfort his mother and aunt, and take the reins of the family's affairs, the funeral was the end of a certain phase of his life, and he found that he was anxious to progress to the next.

"You're sure you'll be all right?" Mr. Archer asked Gwen. The other mourners had already found their carriages, and Robert had bid his mother goodbye. But Regina and her parents remained. "We can arrange for portage."

"That won't be necessary, father, really," Gwen said, leaning in to give him a kiss on the cheek. "Mr. Sheraton and I can bring my trunks and Regina's things. His steward has been at the hall for some days now. Everything's settled."

"I shall take good care of her, Mr. Archer," Robert assured him. "You have my word. We shall return to Renwick tonight."

Gwen bid her family goodbye, and Robert helped her into his carriage, before climbing up himself. Once inside, he rapped on the roof. "To Dredthorne," he called up to the driver.

With a quick check through the back window to assure himself that no one could see them, he joined Gwen on her seat. It was the first time they'd truly been alone since...finding Christopher waiting for them in the library.

He immediately framed her face with his hands and tenderly kissed her mouth. As though time had stood still, she responded in kind. It was as if they'd never been parted. When he released her, they both took in a sharp breath.

"How I've wanted to do that," he breathed.

"It felt like an eternity," she said at the same time.

Reassurance washed through him. As much as he'd looked forward to this moment, he'd worried over it as well. It had occurred to him that Gwen might have a change of heart once she was home, safe with Regina and their parents. Her sister had suffered so cruelly at the hands of his brother, and almost been killed by him herself. But now as she sat smiling beside him, he knew that his fears had been unfounded.

"I've asked Thackery to examine the skeleton that we found in the secret room," he said.

Smiling, she took his hand on her lap. "Oh Robert, what a wonderful idea. I would so like to understand what happened to her."

"I feel we must," he said, nodding. "As you say, it is our duty, not just to her, but also to ourselves."

With that, they nestled against each other, hands clasping hands, and settled in for the ride.

## CHAPTER 18

*D*redthorne loomed before them once more, but this time Gwen was not alone. She had Robert to keep her company and to keep the darkness at bay. Even so, the sight of the grand old hall sent a shiver down her spine.

Even over the sound of the horse hooves on the brick drive, she heard Robert sigh.

"Me too," she said, hugging his arm. "I don't want to be here either. But we'll get our luggage together, and then we'll leave." And get on with our lives, she thought.

"It's strange to think of how I once scoffed at the curse," he said, just as the carriage rolled up in front of the house.

In a moment of déjà vu, a footman

dashed forward. But rather than help her from her rig, he lowered the footstep and opened the door. Robert got out first, and then helped her down. Arm in arm, they ascended the steps and approached the entry together.

"Miss Archer," said a familiar voice. "May I be the first to welcome you back to Dredthorne Hall?"

Gwen turned to see Parks among a small army of other servants.

"Parks!" she exclaimed. Though she knew her station and his should prevent a show of affection, she couldn't help herself. She ran to him, clutched his shoulders, and put her cheek briefly to his. "You look wonderful."

For several seconds, he could only dither and make sputtering sounds. "Miss Gwen," he said finally. "It is...um... wonderful to see you too."

She held him at arm's length for a moment, examining him. "Have you fully recovered?" she said, looking at the scar on his brow before letting him go.

"Yes, Miss. Thanks to you and the master."

Robert stepped forward. "How go the preparations?"

"Very well, sir." He indicated the constant flow of servants carrying trunks, baskets, and bundles to the waiting coaches. "We've almost finished."

"Good," Robert said. "Gwen and I will just have one more look around the old place."

"Very good, sir," he said with a little bow. "Oh, sir, I almost forgot." He took an envelope from the hall table. "This arrived for you yesterday from Dr. Thackery."

Robert opened the envelope and unfolded the letter as Gwen went to his side and they read it together.

"A skull fracture is what killed her," he said.

"Possibly from a fall," she finished, and looked up at him. "Possibly from a fall that was helped with a little push?"

"I wouldn't doubt it," he said. "She obviously fell hard enough to drive her earring into the wall."

"He also says there's no known family," Robert said. "The usual thorough Thackery." He folded the letter and tucked it back into the envelope. "But I'd hoped she might find rest with her people."

"What the doctor can't tell us," Gwen said, "is who might have pushed her."

Slowly they made their way past the stream of servants, stopping at the library. Fresh paint on the ceiling and new drapes at the windows made it seem as though a fire had never happened. Canvas cloths, some worn and discolored, had been draped over all the tables, desks, and chairs. It was like a library of ghostly furniture now. She stood close to Robert, clinging to his arm.

"I can hardly believe this is where I nearly lost you," she whispered.

"Nearly lost me?" he said. "I'm afraid that would have been in front of the bacon skillet."

Though she laughed, she heard the tension in his voice. "Come to the dining room," she said, tugging him along. "I want to see the secret library."

But as soon as they entered, she wished they hadn't. Everything had been cleaned up and put away. Like the library, the furniture had been covered. But more than that, all of the journals had simply been stacked on the shelves instead of being properly arranged. She should have known better than to expect more. The servants wouldn't have known that each had its own place and its own special meaning.

Secretly she'd hoped that she could have one last peek at Mrs. Thorne's journals. But now, that was not to be. Instead she drifted from shelf to shelf, trailing her fingers along the leather spines.

Robert came to her side and they held hands as she slowly surveyed the little library that had been her solace.

He leaned in close to her, his hand in the small of her back. "I can see to the luggage," he said. "You can stay here if you like."

"*No*," she said, before quickly calming herself. She hugged his strong arm and looked into the midnight black of his eyes. "I mean we're together now. We do this together."

He covered her hand with his, warming it and her. "Then I shall stay by your side here, until you are ready."

"I'm ready now," she said. When he

paused and gave her an inquiring look, she squeezed his arm. "Truly. We can go upstairs."

They took the stairs slowly, arm in arm, and Gwen found that the higher they ascended the tighter she gripped him. As they looked down on the new step that Parks had substituted for the sabotaged step, Robert wound his arm around her waist, but neither of them said anything. There was no trace of where Christopher had shot himself, the blood cleaned away and the marble damaged by the musket ball replaced.

But when they mounted the top of the steps, Robert looked up and Gwen followed his gaze. Lodged in the ceiling panel was the projectile from the first pistol. It had escaped even Parks' notice. Robert's grasp of her became fractionally stronger, but again, there didn't seem to be words—at least ones they hadn't already said.

Along the dark hallway, all the doors had been closed.

"Oh," she whispered softly, disappointed

yet again. Perhaps they shouldn't have come after all.

"Let's try the knob anyway," he suggested. As they stood in front of the bedchamber that she had once occupied, Robert reached out his hand, turned the knob, and to her astonishment, pushed the door open.

He beamed at her. "After you, Miss Archer."

As below, all the furnishings had been draped with cloth, but Gwen recognized each one. She went to the chair and desk where she'd spent time reflecting on the thoughts of the Thornes, and wondering what had become of Miss Wilson. There was the chest of drawers and the dressing table. Beyond in the dressing room she knew was the secret door and dusty passage, and she wondered if anyone would ever enter them again.

She heard Robert close the door as she continued her slow circumnavigation, until finally she ended at the bed. He stole up behind her and slipped his arms around her waist. She closed her eyes, reveling in the delicious warmth of his embrace and the feel of his hard chest pressing into her back.

He put his mouth next to her ear. "Do you remember the first night we spent in this room?"

"Yes," she whispered, resting her hands on his arms. "How could I forget?"

As his lips grazed her neck, she tilted her head sideways to permit him more room. His breath was soft, seeming to float down the front of her throat and over her chest.

"I've thought of nothing else," he murmured against her skin.

Even as a familiar warmth began to grow in her belly, Gwen tried to think rationally. "The servants," she whispered harshly. "They might–"

"They're finished here," he said. His lips paused on her neck. "If you want me to stop–"

"*No*," she breathed. "I don't think I could bear it."

In the next instant he hiked her skirts up around her waist, in one smooth movement, causing her to gasp. She knew she was bare to him, but the slither of his hands to the front of her hips pushed that thought from her mind. Instead, she wriggled backward, pushing herself against him, and was rewarded with his moan.

"Oh, Gwen," he murmured. As she leaned forward and put her hands on the bed, his back arched over her. "Yes, that's it." He kissed the nape of her neck. "My sweet, Gwen."

His fingers slid through her netherhair and to her already wet opening, spreading her as a new heat blossomed under his deft touch. Slowly he circled the pearl of her delight in a slow rhythmic motion, making her clench as her hips tried to follow his movement. Over and over she moved with him, brushing the erection in his trousers with her bare bottom. As fire blazed into her belly, Robert grunted. She could feel his hand behind her, unbuttoning his trousers.

Then, when she thought his clever fingers would finally drive her mad, the engorged dome of his cockhead pushed against her opening. Her nipples puckered against her chemise, as her hands bunched the cloth on the bed so hard she thought she might tear it.

Her hips bucked backwards, trying to urge him inside her. He timed his thrust so perfectly that she almost cried out, but instead bit her lower lip. Her opening fluttered wildly around him as he pushed his hard length into her core. He withdrew and thrust again, then again. Gripping her mound as he massaged her pearl, he pulled her back to him, their bodies thudding together.

"*Oh, yes, Robert,*" she gasped.

He thickened inside her just as she bore down on him with a clench so savage she thought it might rend her in two.

"Ah!" he groaned, as passion exploded within her, flooding into her belly, her nipples, and to her very fingertips.

Wild fireworks of ecstasy burst behind her closed eyes, as he jerked inside her, and flooded her with his seed. Over and over she milked him, their bodies perfectly slotted together, rocking in time. He jetted again, his chest heaving against her back, as he held her tightly against him. Only after some moments did they manage to quell the aftershocks of their quick coupling. Exhausted, she fell onto the bed, and

Robert with her. Gently, he lifted her up onto the mattress so she could lay on her side. He lay behind her, cupping her body with his.

Again his lips found the side of her neck. "I love you, my dear Gwen," he murmured against her skin.

"I love you, too," she murmured.

He sighed then, and she heard the utter contentment that she felt. They lay like that in languid silence, until the faint sounds of servants' voices and carts being wheeled drifted up from below.

"It's time," he said, getting up from behind her.

As he buttoned his trousers, she stood and straightened her skirts.

"One more thing about Miss Wilson," he said. "There is the matter of the jewels that she left behind. I believe it would only be proper to offer them to you as compensation for the suffering that Christopher caused."

Astonished, she stared at him. "They're worth a small fortune." She shook her head. "I'm afraid I cannot."

He'd been brushing something from his

coat sleeve, but stopped. "What? But she had no family–"

She held up her hand. "I cannot take them, but I will accept them on my sister's behalf, as her dowry. She deserves to find a man who appreciates her and will take care of her."

Though he didn't seem pleased, he nodded and went to the door, "As you say then. They shall be Regina's."

"But Robert?" she said.

He stopped with his hand on the doorknob. "Yes?"

"I wonder if you would still be willing to marry a penniless woman who simply adores you?"

"*Gwen*," he exclaimed, rushing back to her. He picked her up at the waist, beaming up at her. "You have made me the happiest of men."

She cupped his radiant face with her hands. "It's only fitting, since I am the happiest of women."

Without another word, they raced down the stairs. As she suspected, the carts and coaches were all loaded. Robert locked the entry and then helped her into their waiting carriage. As he settled into the seat next to her, she looked back at the hall.

Dredthorne's curtain-shrouded windows seemed to be watching them, like dark, unblinking eyes. It stood like an impassive sentinel as the last of the daylight faded and an evening breeze rose to scatter the dead leaves around its steps. As the carriage departed, the chill wind rose higher and Gwen could swear that it carried with it a sound—like soft, muffled sobbing.

*Mistress of Sins (Dredthorne Hall Book 3)*

Excerpt

## CHAPTER ONE

A familiar shriek from outside the sitting room made Jennet Reed set down her tea cup and watch the door, resigned to the knowledge that it would soon fling open. Outside the window providing pale sunlight for her morning tea, curls of dying leaves drifted past on a brisk October breeze. All around Reed Park the gardeners would spend the day clearing out the last of the sparse garden beds and gather bulbs for winter storage. Since rising early usually allowed Jennet to enjoy her cozy spot alone for the first hours of the day, she felt rather annoyed.

Rapid footsteps followed the cry, and then Margaret Reed entered with the speed of a woman being hounded by an angry mob. Short, plump and swaddled in a pink velvet dressing gown, she clutched a crumpled paper, which she waved like a flag of frantic surrender.

"Oh, Jennet, oh my dear." Her mother's loose silver-blonde ringlets bobbed wildly around her pale face as she hurried over to the settee, enveloping it with her violet scent. "I found the most detestable missive in amongst the notes and cards that came yesterday. We will be cursed."

"Again?" Jennet drew Margaret down beside her and took the note from her trembling hands. She read over the brief, unsigned message before she looked into her mother's terrified pale blue eyes. "Mama, this is an invitation. Someone wishes me to attend an All Hallows' Eve masquerade at Dredthorne Hall."

"It says that a curse will be cast over us." Her mother stabbed a finger at the paper.

"Unless you go to that monstrous place on that evil night, where I am sure you will be murdered, and I left to die in my old age, bereft and alone."

"Nonsense." That pronouncement caused Margaret to burst into tears. Jennet sighed and searched for her handkerchief.

Allowing her mother to weep for a few moments seemed judicious; Margaret had always been highly-strung and easily distressed, and after an uneventful month likely needed the respite. Once Jennet heard the first hiccup of abating sobs she gently mopped up her mother's tears and made her a cup of too-sweet tea. Then she tackled the contents of the note.

"No one wishes us ill, Mama," she assured Margaret. "Curses are not real, you know this. Mr. Branwen explained that to you in great detail when we broached the subject with him."

"What could a vicar know of the misery that haunts our name?" her mother demanded, wringing the now-damp handkerchief. "Has all of *his* family died while still young? Did *he* lose his dear Papa even before he was born? Was *he* abandoned at the altar on *his* wedding day?"

And there, Jennet thought, was the story of her life in just three questions. Aside from her and her widowed mother, all of their family had died, most of them in their prime. Margaret never cared to be reminded of the reckless, stubborn streak every Reed possessed along with the family's auburn tresses and green eyes. That tempestuous flaw had contributed to those early demises, including her father's. He'd gone off to die fighting the French only a few months after marrying and impregnating Margaret.

Eighteen years later . . .

*No.* Jennet would not think about the most ridiculous chapter in her own rather dull saga. She had sworn never to waste another moment thinking about that bounder, that scoundrel, that deceitful, heartless *beast* of a man.

"Mama," she said, using a firm tone she usually reserved for cheeky footmen and over-curious villagers, "We are not being cursed. I daresay it is a joke in poor taste, nothing more."

"Who would do such a monstrous thing?" Margaret demanded.

"Someone who wishes me to attend so that I might amuse their guests." Jennet already suspected just who that might be. "I imagine they wished to make the invitation seem appropriate to the occasion."

"By cursing us?" her mother shrieked, and then pressed her hand to her brow. "Oh, this will end me now, surely. My head pounds with such violence. Where is Debny? She must send for Dr. Mallory before it is too late."

Since they had reached the second act in Margaret's hysterics, Jennet eyed the door again. Her mother's lady's maid came in a moment later, as Debny knew to wait in the hall until she heard her name needed. With the skill of much practice she coaxed Margaret upstairs to her bed chamber. Her assurances of a soothing tisane, a headache powder and a summons for the village doctor did much more than Jennet could to calm her mistress. Their housekeeper then came in to apologize for leaving the post unattended; she had been in the kitchen going over the week's menus with their cook.

"Do not blame yourself, Mrs. Holloway," Jennet said as she folded the invitation and tucked it in her reticule. "Mama hasn't been distressed for at least a fortnight, so she sought an excuse. Do ask Cook to prepare some light broth for her luncheon, and keep the herbals brewing until the doctor arrives."

The housekeeper nodded as she handed over the rest of the post. "I beg your pardon, Miss, but the butcher's lad mentioned that the Tindalls returned from London yesterday."

"That is welcome news." And a chance to escape her mother's latest bout of agitation, Jennet thought as she rose from the settee. "Please have Barton to ready the rig."

After looking in on her mother, Jennet changed from her morning muslin to a dark green walking dress, and donned a brown hooded wool cloak. While not as fashionable as a spencer jacket, the cloak would keep her warm on the chilly drive over to Tindall House. Margaret would scold her for dressing and driving herself, but Jennet preferred self-reliance over playing the genteel lady. Besides being cursed and jilted at the altar, she had now reached a spinster's age of seven and twenty. No one besides her mother much cared what she did.

Going to the Tindall estate gave Jennet time to enjoy the palette of autumn, which had painted most of Renwick in myriad fiery colors. The fields remained green, and patches of white and purple heather daubed the hillsides, but the trees had gone crimson, gold and apricot. Some of the largest oaks and ashes looked as countless tiny flames blazed from their branches . Despite the damp chill of the morning air, Jennet preferred this time of year to any other in the countryside. Summer's bounty had been harvested, and the snows had yet to arrive. It seemed the perfect season.

*That was why you chose to marry in October, so the church could be adorned in autumnal splendor, to match your garnet hair and witch's eyes.*

"I did not marry," Jennet told the errant thought as she guided the horse up the winding drive to her friend's home. "I am not a witch."

*You bewitch me,* a deep voice chided from her memory.

Once more Jennet saw herself in her wedding gown, standing in the church while a younger Mr. Branwen comforted a noisily weeping Margaret and hundreds of guests whispered and stared at her. She had been like a pillar of salt, frozen for all eternity halfway to an empty altar where her marriage would not be taking place. Later she would feel the humiliation, the despair, and the deep and abiding hatred of the man who had so thoroughly ruined her. In that moment, however, all she could think was how she had never anticipated this, not once. She believed she had been loved as much as she had loved.

*Never again.*

• • • • •

Buy *Mistress of Sins (Dredthorne Hall Book 3)*

# DEDICATION

*For Mr. H.*

# COPYRIGHT